"You really don't work at anything?"

Sienna's gaze flicked from his clearly expensive house and back to him.

"Life's short," Jack said flippantly. "I live for pleasure."

Suspicion clouded her expression. "Then how do you get money?"

"I'm not a drug dealer. Nothing illegal is going on."

"But you must have worked at some point." She leaned on the porch railing, studying him. "Are you really content with just hobbies?"

He sensed she wanted to like him. He wasn't being egotistical to think that. And he was attracted to her. Yet it was clear she couldn't help judging him. Self-indulgent. Lazy. Hedonistic. He could almost hear the pronouncements flowing through her mind. Those qualities weren't what she, a doctor, stood for.

"I'm not a bad person," he said, attempting to make a joke of it. "In fact, you and I operate by the same code—first, do no harm."

"You don't do *harm* by having a job."

"I had a job once." He shrugged. "I got tired of it."

It had been a great job, too. One he loved. But he'd screwed up. And Leanne had paid the price.

Dear Reader,

My life, knock on wood, has so far been free of major misfortune. When I hear or read about people whose lives have been taken from joy to tragedy after a fatal accident, it tears at my heart. They will be living with the physical and emotional consequences of their trauma for years to come.

How do they cope? What do they endure? Family and friends play a major role in helping people heal. But sometimes that's not enough. I wish I could give everyone out there a happy ending, but as a writer all I can do is give my characters a happy-ever-after and hope that their stories will touch hearts and give hope.

Jack Thatcher, hero of *Her Great Expectations*, is beloved by his family, friends and community. Three years after the death of his wife in a plane crash, Jack appears to be coping but inside, guilt and grief have him in their grip. It takes an outsider, Dr. Sienna Maxwell, to see that Jack is still broken. She challenges rather than coddles him, forcing him to confront his darkest fears and, finally, to heal.

Her Great Expectations is the first book in the Summerside Stories series. These stories are about siblings Jack, Renita and Lexie, and their lives and loves in a small Australian town by the sea. They're about family, friendship and community, all the things that make the world go around.

I love to hear from readers. You can email me at www.joankilby.com or write to me c/o Harlequin Enterprises Limited, 225 Duncan Mill Road, Don Mills, ON, M3B 3K9 Canada.

Joan Kilby

Her Great Expectations

Joan Kilby

TORONTO • NEW YORK • LONDON
AMSTERDAM • PARIS • SYDNEY • HAMBURG
STOCKHOLM • ATHENS • TOKYO • MILAN • MADRID
PRAGUE • WARSAW • BUDAPEST • AUCKLAND

Recycling programs
for this product may
not exist in your area.

ISBN-13: 978-0-373-71681-4

HER GREAT EXPECTATIONS

This edition published by arrangement with Harlequin Books S.A.

For questions and comments about the quality of this book please contact us at Customer_eCare@Harlequin.ca.

www.eHarlequin.com

Printed in U.S.A.

ABOUT THE AUTHOR

Joan Kilby lives in a small seaside village in Australia very much like the town of Summerside in *Her Great Expectations.* Many of the geographical features in the story are real and an inspiration to Joan. She loves walking along the creek with her Jack Russell terrier, Toby. And she, her husband and their three grown children enjoy warm summer evenings on the deck with a glass of wine and a barbecue. Watching the rainbow lorikeets flit home among the gum trees as the sun sets over the bay is just about as idyllic as it gets.

Books by Joan Kilby

HARLEQUIN SUPERROMANCE

777—A FATHER'S PLACE
832—TEMPORARY WIFE
873—SPENCER'S CHILD
941—THE CATTLEMAN'S BRIDE
965—THE SECOND PROMISE
1030—CHILD OF HIS HEART
1076—CHILD OF HER DREAMS
1114—CHILD OF THEIR VOWS
1212—HOMECOMING WIFE
1224—FAMILY MATTERS
1236—A MOM FOR CHRISTMAS
1324—PARTY OF THREE
1364—BEACH BABY
1437—NANNY MAKES THREE
1466—HOW TO TRAP A PARENT

To Victoria Curran, my wonderful editor,
whose insight, talent and hard work
help make my books the best they can be.
She hauls me back when I go over the top,
"roughs" me up when I get too soft and
gives me a much-needed pat on the back
when I dig deep and make it "real."
Thank you, Victoria!

CHAPTER ONE

DR. SIENNA MAXWELL WAS trying hard to ignore the ridiculously good-looking man on the other side of the greengrocer. Then a burst of rich male laughter mingled with an elderly lady's girlish giggle made her glance up again. Casually elegant in a thin black V-necked sweater and tan pants, he could have been George Clooney's younger brother with his thick rumpled dark hair, warm brown eyes and engaging smile. As she watched, he made a kiwifruit appear from behind the ear of the pink-cheeked, white-haired granny who was, unbelievably, flirting with him.

Tucking back a long corkscrew of red hair, Sienna focused on the fat white bulbs and feathery green fronds of fresh fennel. Even though she had no idea how to cook them, she placed two in her shopping cart while still taking note of the man's every movement.

He placed the kiwifruit in the woman's basket, gently squeezed her shoulder and moved on, only to be stopped by a hearty greeting from a man with a beefy red face. Relaxed and cheerful, the Clooney look-alike cocked a hip and leaned on his cart to settle in for a chat as if he had all the time in the world.

A warning vibration burred in Sienna's jacket pocket—her phone alarm giving her a ten-minute reminder to get back to the clinic for her first patient of the afternoon. She'd rushed out during her lunch break to pick up a few specialty items she needed for a Thai curry because Glyneth and Rex were coming out from the city. Sienna had rashly promised her friends a special dinner, boasting she was going to cook it herself.

Distracted by snatches of the man's smooth deep voice, she found her gaze drifting across the store again. Now a woman in her thirties towing two young children had stopped to say a few words to him. While they chatted a retired couple waved and called out a greeting. He seemed to know everyone in town.

In stark contrast to her own situation. When she'd moved to the village she'd had a romantic notion of hosting casual dinner parties. Two months in, she still didn't know anyone she could invite over for coffee, much less spend Saturday evening with. She was simply too busy working to find the time to make friends. Oh, she had Oliver, but he was spending more and more time with his mates from school.

Sienna remembered she had a grocery list and checked it. Kaffir lime leaves, whatever *those* were. As she turned her cart toward the Asian food section, she cast a last covert glance at the dark-haired man. She didn't know if she wanted to *be* him, or *do* him. Not that she was in the habit of "doing" anyone. At least not in a long time. But there was something about this guy that was stirring her dormant hormones to life. How was it she'd been in Summerside for three months and never run into him before?

Dark eyes set in a tanned masculine face met her gaze across the central display of cut flowers. A small smile played around the corners of a mouth with just the right combination of angles and curves to be ultrasexy.

Heat rose in her cheeks at being caught staring. Sienna blindly pushed her cart forward, noting with clinical detachment her rush of adrenaline and increased heart rate. *Get a grip.* She was an adult, not a teenager. A doctor, with loftier thoughts than rampant sex among the squashes.

Abandoning her quest for lime leaves, she grabbed a plastic bag and filled it with whatever was in front of her. Just when her pulse was back to normal and she'd regained her composure, that deep low voice sounded not three feet away. He'd crossed the shop and was exchanging pleasantries with the woman standing next to her. Sienna forced herself not to glance over, but her nerve endings prickled with awareness. Then the female shopper moved along and nothing but two feet of air separated her and George Clooney's brother.

That was when she spied the Kaffir lime leaves on the shelf. Grateful for the distraction, she stretched her fingers out. Clooney reached for the same packet at the same time. Their fingertips touched. She yanked her hand back and the plastic container tumbled to the floor. She crouched to pick it up.

So did he, getting there first. Holding out the lime leaves, he said, "Here you go."

"Thanks." Meeting his gaze made the warmth rise in her cheeks. She scrambled to her feet before he could offer assistance, and, flustered, scanned the shelf. "There are more."

"Plenty," he said, dropping another packet into his cart. "Are you making curry?"

Sienna tucked back more wayward curls bent on escaping her loose ponytail. Recalling the complicated recipe she'd cut out of a magazine, she nodded. "Thai green curry. With chicken."

"You'll also need galangal, green chilies..." As he spoke he took the items from the shelf, piling them up in one broad hand. "Fresh coriander, ginger..."

Eyeing the unfamiliar ingredients, she was starting to wish she'd picked an easier dish to learn on. "No, please, I won't take those. I wanted to be adventurous, but I think I've bitten off more than I can chew. I've got a jar of curry paste I bought at the supermarket as backup."

"The bottled stuff is never as good." He hesitated, but only for a second. "Would you like to come to my house for dinner tonight? I'm having a few people over. You can be adventurous without all the chopping."

Sienna chewed on her lip. *Say yes, you idiot. Are you kidding? I don't even know him.* Just in time she remembered Glyneth and Rex. "Thank you, but I'm busy."

"I don't blame you for being cautious," he conceded. "But you can ask anybody—I'm a good guy."

"I don't doubt it after seeing you work this shop." The phone in her pocket vibrated again. Five minutes. "If you'll excuse me, I have to get back to work."

"Drinks are at seven o'clock. We don't usually sit down to eat until nine. So, will you come?"

"Seriously, I've already got plans."

"Next Saturday, then. Mark it down in your diary."

Sienna couldn't help laughing. "Do you have a dinner party every weekend?"

"I'm not sure if it's worthy of that title," he said with a shrug. "I make a big meal and whoever shows up scrambles for a place. If there are too many people I haul out the card table."

What a contrast to the dinner parties she and Anthony used to give in Melbourne. Formal events, planned weeks in advance with elaborate place settings straight out of *Gourmet* magazine. Catered mostly, because she never had time to cook and because among their circle of friends the competition to provide the fanciest food was so steep it was completely beyond her. Name cards, floral decorations, three different wineglasses and twice as many forks. She had never been relaxed enough to enjoy them. And she'd ended up positively hating them after she'd found out what Anthony and her so-called friend Erica had got up to in the pantry between courses.

Her smile faded. She still couldn't get her head around the fact that her marriage had broken up. That sort of thing wasn't supposed to happen in her perfect world. "I have to go."

"I'm Jack." He pulled out his wallet and withdrew a card, which he pressed into her hand. "Here's my address in case you change your mind."

She glanced at the card. Jack Thatcher, Linden Avenue. Before she could reply or tell him her name, an elderly man—obviously hard of hearing, and holding a cane—spoke in a loud voice, one gnarled hand cupped behind his ear. "How ya going, Jack? The missus wants to know why you haven't been around for a slice of her lemon cake lately."

Sienna backed away, sliding his card into the side

pocket of her purse. She hurried through the checkout and out of the shop. After crossing at the pedestrian walkway, she continued up the street, past the pet store and the chain grocery toward the clinic on Main Street at the end of the two-block commercial area.

Although the sun was still above the treetops, a light spring breeze made her glad of her jacket; here on the peninsula it was always a few degrees cooler than the city. But the tiny coastal town felt right for her at this point in her life. Professionally she'd made a significant career advance in becoming head doctor at the busy Summerside Clinic. And now her encounter with Jack Thatcher had left a pleasurable buzz in her veins, as though good times were just around the corner.

Bev, the well-groomed fiftysomething receptionist, was clacking away at the computer when Sienna entered.

Sienna greeted her and went through into the area behind the reception desk. There she paused and eyed Bev speculatively. Summerside was a small town, only around five thousand people. The gregarious receptionist could likely give her some background on the man she'd just met.

"Oh, Bev," she said casually. "Do you by any chance know Jack Thatcher?"

Bev stopped typing and swiveled her chair to face Sienna, unconsciously lifting her bejeweled fingers to groom her sleek blond bob. "Everyone knows Jack," she said with a little sigh. "He's famous for his dinner parties."

"Is he married?"

"Widower." Bev glanced around to see if anyone was close enough to hear, then lowered her voice a notch.

"His wife died in a light plane crash a few years ago. Terrible tragedy." She tilted her head to regard Sienna. "Why do you ask?"

"No reason. I met him in the shop just now." She never would have guessed there was heartbreak hiding behind that affable smile.

"A word of warning." Bev cast a knowing eye at Sienna. "Plenty of women have made a play for him, but he never dates. Ever. They say he's still in love with his wife."

"I'm not *interested* in him," Sienna replied quickly. "He seemed very friendly, that's all."

"He is friendly! With everyone. It doesn't matter if you're old, young, rich or poor, Jack would give you the shirt off his back. He's a great guy. He's just not a good prospect, if you know what I mean."

"He invited me to dinner tonight."

"Really?" Bev said, looking interested.

Bev would have gossiped all day long, but Sienna gave her a gotta-go smile and carried her shopping into the staff room. She hung her jacket in the closet and put the groceries in a corner of the kitchen counter where they'd be all right for a couple of hours. Peeking into the bag, she shook her head. She'd left the shop without everything she'd gone for. And ended up with a whole lot of items she didn't even recall putting in her basket.

All because a charming man with a smile like George Clooney's had locked eyes with her across a busy shop.

JACK WIPED THE SWEAT from his forehead with the hem of his T-shirt as he jogged up to his parents' single-story brick house. Knocking twice, he opened the door. "Anybody home?"

"Hello, darling." Hetty bustled out to greet him.

"Mother?" He did a double take. Her habitual attire was slacks and cardigans, her dyed blond hair styled in a neat chin-length pageboy. Today was the first time he'd seen her since returning from three months in Queensland. Now she wore flowing silky pants and a loose muslin tunic. Her hair, now gray, was chopped short.

She went to hug him but pulled back. "You're all sweaty."

"What did you do to your hair?" Jack propped his hands on his hips and walked around her in a circle.

Hetty brushed her fingers through the spiky cut. "Do you like it?"

"It's…different."

"I've decided to *own* my gray hair." She smiled, her clear blue eyes shining. "To be my age, my authentic self."

"Really? Who have you been pretending to be till now?"

"Oh, Jack!"

"I'm kidding." Jack laid an arm loosely over her shoulders. "I think it's cool."

"How was your trip?" she asked, smiling up at him. "You've been gone forever, it seems."

"Excellent. I highly recommend the tropics as a place to spend the winter." He let her go and followed her through the arched doorway into the lounge room. Steve was sitting in his recliner with a beer, staring out the window at the horse paddocks opposite. Smedley, his Jack Russell terrier, lay curled at his feet. "Hey, Dad."

"Jack," Steve grunted, but didn't get up.

Hetty huffed out a sigh. "He just sits there hour after hour, doing nothing. Sometimes I think we never should have sold the farm."

"How are *you* doing?"

"I'm fine. More than fine. Come into the kitchen. I just made brownies." Leading the way, she glanced over her shoulder. "How did Bogie take to living on a sailboat?"

"As if he was born to it," Jack said. "I came in to port every night and made sure he had a walk."

"So...did you meet anyone while you were away?"

"No." Not while he'd been away. Even as he spoke his mind flashed to the woman in the grocery shop.

"That's funny." She frowned. "I had this hunch."

"Sorry, your mother's intuition is faulty this time."

Jack followed her into the small sunny kitchen permeated with the smell of fresh baking. A basket of wet laundry sat by the back door waiting to be hung on the clothesline.

"Steve keeps complaining I never bake anymore, so I gave in for once," Hetty said, slicing a row of brownies.

"He likes his sweets." Jack pinched a bar and took a bite. "With good reason. This is delicious."

"It's time for his annual checkup, but he keeps putting it off," Hetty went on. "His old doctor retired and he doesn't want to 'break in' a new one. I think he's scared the doctor will tell him to lose weight and get healthy."

"Do you and Dad want to come for dinner on Saturday?" Jack asked. "Renita and Lexie will be there."

"I'm going on a two-week retreat at the meditation center," Hetty said. "But your father can. It would be a relief to know he's not just sitting here brooding."

"Meditation, huh? This really is a new you."

Hetty's eyes shut. A beatific smile transformed her face, and when she opened her eyes again she radiated calm. "I feel so peaceful, I can't tell you. I wish Steve would try it." Her smile faded and her expression turned wistful. "He's not supportive. I think he feels threatened."

"He'll get used to it." Jack brushed the crumbs off his hands over the sink. "I'll go talk to him."

Jack put another piece of brownie on a plate and took it to his father in the lounge room. He noticed a plate with chocolate crumbs on the side table next to the recliner. And Steve's stomach bulging over his waistband. Hetty was right—he'd put on a few pounds since Jack had seen him last. "Here you go, Dad. What's up?"

Steve took the brownie and had a bite. "Your mother's turned lesbian."

Jack fought back a laugh. "It's just a haircut." He lowered himself onto the dark green brocade couch opposite and reached out to pat Smedley, who'd trotted over.

"It's more than a haircut," Steve growled. "She's joined a cult. According to the pamphlets she brings home, they're celibate up there at the retreat center."

"Celibate is hardly the same as lesbian," Jack said, shaking his head.

"Who knows what she gets up to with those people in white robes," Steve said. "I just know she's not here with me."

"You should develop some interests of your own," Jack suggested.

Ignoring that, Steve polished off the brownie. "And she's hardly ever around to cook dinner."

"Come on, Dad. You can look after yourself." This grumpiness was out of character for Steve. *He's afraid,* Jack thought. Afraid of getting old, of becoming redundant.

Of losing Hetty.

Steve dabbed at the crumbs on the plate. "I expected the girls to take her side, but not you."

"I came to invite you to dinner on Saturday," Jack said, sidestepping the issue. The last thing he wanted was to get involved in his parents' marriage problems.

"Football's on that night. Will you be watching?"

"Probably not."

"Then forget it." Steve took off his steel-framed glasses and peered at the lenses. "Damn things are always blurry."

"Are you feeling okay? I hear you're going to see the doctor soon."

"There's nothing wrong with me," Steve said, polishing his glasses on the hem of his shirt. "I'm fit as a fiddle."

Jack waited, expecting a qualifier, but none came. "That's fine, but you should get that checkup. Why don't you come jogging with me sometime?"

"No, thanks. Too energetic for me." Steve lifted his beer to drink, but it was empty. "Hetty! Can you bring me another cold one?"

There was no answer.

With difficulty he pushed himself out of his chair and

unbent, one hand supporting his lower back. "Where is that woman? She's never around when I need her."

"She's probably outside hanging up the washing. I'll get you a beer." But Steve was already shuffling to the kitchen. Sighing, Jack glanced at his watch. "I've got to go. I'll catch you later, Dad."

"OLIVER, I'M HOME." Sienna glanced at her watch. Six o'clock. She was running late. She dropped her bag of groceries on the dark green granite counter in her small, efficient kitchen. Leafing through the envelopes she'd collected from the mailbox on her way in, she listened for her son's reply. Electricity bill, junk mail, letter from the high school… "Oliver, are you here?"

"I'm in my room." His voice cracked on every second syllable. "On the computer."

Leaving the groceries and the mail for the moment, Sienna went to the low bookshelf in the breakfast nook and took out the local map. She didn't have time for this, but she was curious to find out exactly where Jack Thatcher lived.

Linden Avenue, she discovered, was on the southern outskirts of town about two miles from the village center. There the houses bordered paddocks where cattle and horses grazed. Her house was a couple of miles north of the town, in an older part of Summerside. She wasn't likely to bump into him while out jogging. Damn.

Sienna closed the map book and went back to the kitchen to start dinner, embarrassed by her foolish preoccupation. If she kept this up, the next thing she knew she'd be driving past his house. She shook her head. That was *so* not going to happen.

She put away the groceries and got the chicken out of the freezer to defrost in the microwave. But like a terrier with a bone, her mind kept going back to Jack and his Thai green curry. If Glyneth and Rex hadn't been coming she could have accepted his invitation. She wouldn't have to even think about cruising slowly past like some creepy stalker—she'd be pulling into his driveway, a welcome guest.

While the chicken thawed, Sienna opened the letter from the school, thinking it was probably a notice of some event. But as she scanned the single page her heart sank. It was from the middle-school coordinator, informing her tersely that Oliver had failed to hand in assignments in three subjects—English, math and biology. Sienna breathed out hard, nostrils flaring. Olly was a smart kid; she shouldn't be getting letters like this about him.

"Oliver!" she yelled loud enough for him to hear her in his room.

"I'm right here." He appeared abruptly in the doorway. He'd changed out of his olive-green-and-gray school uniform into a Billabong T-shirt and blue jeans, and put fresh gel on his thick curly blond hair. He made his way into the kitchen, brushing past her on his way to the cupboard that held the water glasses. At six foot, he was already taller than her by six inches. "What's the matter?"

She shook the letter, rustling the paper. "Mr. Kitzinger says you haven't been turning in assignments."

"Oh." Glass in hand, he edged past her to help himself to water from the tap.

"Well, what do you have to say for yourself?"

He drank a few gulps, then dashed the rest of the water into the sink. "I hate English, my math teacher is crap and I want to drop biology next year."

Alarmed, Sienna rubbed her bare arms, crumpling the letter. She knew Oliver was at an age where interest in school waned, but this was the first time he'd talked about dropping science subjects. "Regardless of how you feel about your teachers or the subjects, the fact is, you have to do the work. If you don't improve your marks, you're never going to be accepted into university."

He slumped against the counter, his eyebrows lowering over his deep-set gray-blue eyes. "Maybe I don't *want* to go to uni."

Sienna felt her blood go cold. "You don't know what you want. You're only fourteen."

"Exactly. I'm only fourteen. So quit planning my life for me." Pushing off the counter, Oliver went into the family room, threw himself onto the couch and switched on the TV.

"Turn if off, please." Sienna waited, silently counting to ten. She got to eight before he did as she asked. "If you want to be a doctor you need to learn good study habits—"

"I *don't* want to be a doctor. You're the one who wants it. We've got enough doctors in this family already—Dad, you, Nanna and Pop."

"When I was your age I didn't think I wanted to be a doctor, either. I changed my mind," Sienna told him. "You'll change your mind, too, when you get older."

"You don't know that," Oliver protested. "You think you know me, but you don't."

She took a breath, planning to say that of course she knew him—he was her son, her baby she'd taken care of since he was born. She knew the birthmark on his back and the way his big toe curved inward, just like hers. She knew he worried about global warming and that he liked comedy shows better than crime dramas.

Then she looked at the great big boy sitting on the couch, staring at her with a mixture of sullenness and anxiety, and her words stopped in her throat. *Did* she know him anymore, really? Oh, he was still her son and all those things about him were still true, but he was changing. Growing up, growing away from her. He was developing muscles and peach fuzz on his chin and a mind of his own. She no longer knew his every thought and feeling, because he no longer blurted them out as soon as he came through the door. All too soon he would be a man. Blink and he'd be gone, leaving home.

She crossed her arms over her tightened stomach. "What…what do you want to do?"

Oliver hunched his broad bony shoulders. "I don't know. Dig ditches, maybe."

Oh, God. Sienna felt the breath stick in her chest. He didn't mean that—he was just trying to push her buttons. And doing a darn good job of it, too. Oliver had been in the gifted class right through primary school. He had so much potential. She had such high hopes for him. The important thing for her right now was not to overreact.

Letting her breath go, she said calmly, "Whatever

you end up doing, it's important that you finish high school. Keep your grades up, take a variety of courses and keep your options open."

"I guess," he said grudgingly, not looking at her.

Now that he was acquiescing, she couldn't resist one more salvo. "Oliver, you know how strongly I feel about education. It's a crime to have the gift of intelligence and talent and not use it to the best of your ability."

"A crime is something that's against the law," said Oliver, ever the nitpicker.

Hands on her hips, Sienna shot back, "In *my* world, not living up to your potential *is* against the law."

Oliver groaned theatrically and pushed his hands through his blond curls.

"I want you to get right in there after dinner and get busy on your homework," Sienna added. "No MSN, no texting your friends—"

"It's Saturday night," Oliver complained. "I'm going to Jason's. I'll do the assignments this weekend."

"Oliver—"

"I promise!"

The microwave was beeping. Sienna went back to the kitchen and removed the thawed chicken. She took out her brand-new wok and got out the chopping board, biting her tongue not to keep haranguing him. "All right. You can go to Jason's, but you will spend the rest of the weekend catching up on your schoolwork." Seconds ticked by. She glanced at him. "Well?"

Finally Oliver said, "Okay." He shuffled his large feet, ruffling the area rug that overlaid the polished hardwood floor. A few more seconds passed. "Do you want to see my solar-powered robot?"

Sienna took another deep breath and released it. "Sure."

Oliver went to his bedroom and came back with a flashlight and a weird-looking contraption made out of a computer disk with half a Ping-Pong ball and two rubber-tipped motors attached to the bottom surface. Wires ran from the motor "legs" through the central hole to an array of light sensors, he explained. The sensors were wired to a small switch and a backup battery pack. Oliver placed the robot on the floor and knelt beside it. He flicked on the switch and shone the flashlight onto the sensors.

Nothing happened.

Oliver's fair skin flushed, the scattered pimples on his chin turning deeper red. He thrust the light closer. "Come on."

"Give it a minute," Sienna said.

Slowly the legs began to move up and down, the rubber tips squeaking backward over the floor. It was the oddest thing Sienna had ever seen. "That's amazing! Did you do that in science?"

"Yeah, we had a special presentation this morning," he said eagerly. "A guy came in and showed us how to make electronic stuff. It was way cool." The robot crashed into the side of the couch and marched frenetically in place until Oliver pulled it away and sent it in another direction. "I need better legs for it, though. And something to make it go in reverse. Jack said the next time he'd bring more controls."

Jack. Could it be the same man? She dismissed the thought. No, it was too much of a coincidence.

She reached out and squeezed Oliver's shoulder.

"You're a smart kid. You've got a scientific mind. You could do anything."

Oliver glanced up at her, his mouth curving uncertainly. She returned his smile with love and pride. Briefly his eyes met hers in naked affection that embarrassed him so much he colored and glanced away.

"Oh, Olly." Flooded with warmth, Sienna reached over and hugged him. He hugged her back briefly, then began to squirm. With a sigh she scrubbed her hand through his hair and reluctantly let him go.

They watched the robot squeak and scrape across the tiles. Meesha, the black cat, dropped from the chair arm where she'd been curled up sleeping and watched the jerking mechanical computer disk with alert interest.

Sienna asked, "Have you talked to your father lately?"

Oliver tensed, then shook his head, pretending all his concentration was on the erratic progress of the robot.

But Sienna could tell she had his attention. "Have you told him yet whether you'll go with him on the ski trip to New Zealand?"

"Why do you want me to go? I'd have to miss a week of school. And the qualifying exam to see if I can go into the advanced math class next year."

"I'll speak to your teacher. We'll work something out."

The robot hit the table leg and stopped. Oliver picked it up and watched the legs give one last flicker. "I don't want to go if *she's* going."

Sienna's jaw tightened, but she strove for an even tone. "Erica's seven months pregnant and not having an easy time. From what Anthony said, I doubt she's going."

Still Oliver hesitated. Sienna didn't want to lecture him again tonight, but neither did she want him to miss this opportunity. "If you want to maintain a good relationship with your dad you need to spend time with him. Every second weekend isn't enough. We agreed that you would have a holiday with him every year."

Oliver glanced up, his eyes searching her face. "Doesn't it bother you? Her, I mean."

Yes, it did. She'd gotten past her initial raw anger and grief, but the hurt lingered. However, she wanted to do what was best for Oliver. "This isn't about me. You don't have to choose sides. You can love us both. You can even—" she swallowed hard "—love Erica."

"*That's* never going to happen." Oliver was silent for a moment, thoughtful. "You really don't mind?"

"No, I don't. I *want* you to go."

He glanced at her as if to make absolutely certain, then his expression gradually brightened as the reality of the trip started to sink in. "Okay. I'll call him now." He hesitated, then hugged her quickly. "Thanks."

As she watched her son scramble to his feet and head for the phone, heat pricked Sienna's eyes. She'd known he was ambivalent about going, but not that his reluctance was out of concern for her feelings. She hated to think of him not going after what he wanted, only to have regrets. That applied to his schoolwork, too, even if he couldn't see it right now.

She got to her feet, glancing once again at her watch. Oh, God. It was six-thirty. Her guests would be here soon and she'd better get busy.

"I COULD HAVE SWORN she was enjoying our conversation, then out of the blue her smile turned sour," Jack said to Bogie as he unloaded groceries onto the kitchen counter. "Do you think it was something I said?"

Bogie's heavy fringed tail wagged in sympathy, but the golden retriever was too busy trawling the tiled floor for spilled crumbs to actually reply.

"It's not like I'm in the habit of stalking women in the vegetable aisles," Jack continued in his one-sided conversation. "But if you'd seen that mess of red curls you'd have crossed the room to talk to her, too."

She looked to be about his age, maybe a little younger, say early to mid-thirties. Designer jeans, good-quality flat leather shoes, crisp white blouse beneath a tailored dark jacket. She could be an upmarket housewife—plentiful in Summerside. Then again, those slender fingers with their just-scrubbed look and short clean nails could belong to a pianist. Or a brain surgeon. All in all, he guessed pianist, but maybe that was simply because he had a thing for Oscar Peterson.

Oscar was on the CD player now, jazzy piano notes bouncing around the kitchen like the dust motes in the last rays of the sun spilling through the large windows overlooking the back garden. Outside, rainbow lorikeets were flitting home to roost in the gum trees, their raucous chatter nearly drowning out the music. Inside the sprawling single-story house, terra cotta tiles and walls of ocher and almond gave off a cozy warm glow. Jack poured himself a glass of red wine and began to cook.

An hour later the aroma of chili, garlic and ginger permeated the kitchen. The first of his guests, his sister

Renita, banged open the front door and called through the house. "Hey, Jack. Come and give me a hand. This box weighs a ton."

He strode out of the kitchen and into a short hallway bordering the lounge room to see his sister, her dark head and curvy round figure almost hidden behind a large cardboard box. He took it out of her arms. "This isn't so heavy. Maybe you need to start lifting weights."

"Ugh, I can't think of anything I'd like less." Renita went ahead of him to the kitchen, her ponytail swinging and her flip-flops slapping on the tiles. She'd changed out of the suit she wore as the loans manager at the local bank and into a sleeveless top and cargo pants.

"I thought you were bringing a date," Jack said.

"He had to go away on business." Over her shoulder she asked, "How was your trip?"

"Let me see… Three months sailing and diving on the Great Barrier Reef? Life doesn't get much better than that."

"Yeah, yeah, don't rub it in," Renita grumbled good-naturedly. "Some of us have to work for a living."

Jack set the box on the counter. "Is there any point in me learning your new guy's name?"

"Probably not. At least *I'm* dating." Renita went to the cupboard for a wineglass and opened the bottle of sauvignon blanc she'd brought. "Hey, have you seen Mum since you've been back? She's cut all her hair off."

"I kind of like it. I'm worried about Dad, though," Jack said. "Ever since he retired he's been so morose. It's been six months and now that Mum's got all these new interests I think he's feeling left behind."

"Did you invite him tonight?" she asked, pouring.

"He'd rather watch the footy." Jack lifted the box flaps to look inside. "What have you got?"

"Ingredients for a Thai seafood appetizer. It's best cooked at the last minute." Renita stirred the wok on the stove and sniffed appreciatively. "Smells good. I saw Sharon at the liquor store. She and Glenn are going to be a bit late. Who else is coming?"

"Lexie, Ron and Diane." Jack stirred the fragrant curry, then dipped a spoon into the coconut-milk broth and tasted. It needed something… Ah, how could he forget? Kaffir lime leaves. He stacked six of the deep green leaves on the chopping block and sliced them into slivers. An image rushed back to him of crouching to retrieve the fallen packet and gazing into a pair of huge gray-green eyes, clear as water. A faint pink blush had stained her pale cream cheeks as he'd shoved the packet into her hands.

Glancing over at his sister, he asked, "Do I come on too strong?"

Renita's eyebrows shot up as she looked at him over her glass of sauvignon blanc. "Okay, spill. Who is she?"

CHAPTER TWO

"WHY DO YOU ASSUME there's a woman?" Jack turned away to sprinkle the chopped leaves into the bubbling curry.

"Because with a man, you wouldn't even think of asking that question. Plus I'm always hoping you'll meet someone." Renita crunched on a prawn cracker from the bowl on the counter. Gently she added, "It's been three years since the accident, Jack. We all loved Leanne, but don't you think it's time to move on? You deserve someone wonderful."

Jack stirred the curry. He and Renita were close, but there were things he hadn't told his sister about the crash. Didn't she get that he'd *tried* to move on? "I asked a woman out today."

Renita lowered her prawn cracker. "Jack, that's wonderful! Are we going to meet her tonight?"

"Don't get excited. She said no." He measured rice and water into the rice cooker and sprinkled in salt. "They always discover my hidden personality defects and scram."

"What's her name?" Renita said, getting back to the point.

"I didn't ask." He was still kicking himself for that oversight. "She's just a woman I met over Kaffir lime leaves in the grocery shop. She must be new around here. I've never seen her before." Or she could have been passing through. An unwelcome thought.

"Did you invite her to dinner?"

"I all but issued a standing invitation for every Saturday night from now till eternity."

"And she declined," Renita deduced. "Any sensible woman would. You should have asked her out for coffee first."

"Yeah, maybe, but I was getting good vibes. Then I mentioned a dinner party and her smile wilted like week-old lettuce."

"Could be she doesn't eat." Renita started taking items out of the box she'd brought. "Was she superskinny?"

"No, she seemed just right," Jack said, thinking back to her soft curves, partly hidden beneath her jacket. Then he shrugged. "Never mind. It was just a spur-of-the-moment thing. You know me—I'd invite the postman for breakfast."

Six months after the crash and fresh out of the hospital, he actually *had* asked the postie in for coffee. Begged, in fact, offering to drive Irwin around on his route to make up for the lost time. It had been one of those days when the walls vibrated with silence and empty rooms echoed with the voices of the dead. Jack had gone a little crazy. He'd probably be in the loony bin right now if Irwin hadn't obligingly drunk three cups of coffee and listened to Jack ramble on. Not that Jack had said anything of significance. He'd yakked about local politics, the weather, anything but his grief and guilt.

The crash had been a turning point for Jack. Before, he'd run a successful light-aircraft charter, rebuilt airplane engines and worked on his own invention, an improved global positioning system for small planes. After the crash he'd walked away from the business, the flying and his broken GPS, now shrouded in plastic in his work shed. He'd had no paid employment for three years. Investments and insurance payouts kept him in groceries, paid the mortgage and financed cheap extended holidays. His family sometimes got after him to go back to work, but mostly they supported whatever he chose to do. Personally, he didn't see a single thing wrong with his lifestyle. Wasn't it everyone's dream to have enough money and leisure to travel and pursue hobbies while they were young enough to enjoy it?

Now Jack made a career out of making sure he was always surrounded by family and friends.

Life was too short to spend it working. As subtext to that motto was another. "Never alone, never lonely." The one thing his mother and sisters would say he lacked was intimacy, but they were women—and women were never content until a man was hooked up for life.

The doorbell rang. Before Jack could react, it rang again. And again. He caught Renita's eye. They burst out laughing and said in unison, "Lexie." Jack didn't bother going down the hall. Lexie would be inside before he got there. The bell was less a request for entry than an announcement of her impending whirlwind arrival.

Sure enough, a moment later their older sister hurried into the kitchen clutching a wine bottle, her shoulder-length curly blond hair swinging behind her as if trying to catch up. Lexie was thirty-eight going on eighteen, and about as responsible as an eight-year-old, but her smile lit a room. "When do we eat? I'm starving."

"Jack's met someone," Renita announced.

"I haven't." Jack shot her a warning frown.

"Who is she?" Lexie squealed, ignoring Jack's denial. She reached for a wineglass, her fingers clean but permanently stained with oil paints. Tonight she'd changed out of the equally stained, loose shirt she wore while working on portraits and into a long Indian cotton skirt and a V-necked T-shirt. A fractured stripe of cobalt-blue curved around her forearm like a tattooed bracelet.

"No one," Jack said firmly.

"A mystery woman who likes to cook," Renita said.

"I'm not sure about that," Jack protested.

"She was after Kaffir lime leaves," Renita pointed out. "Not exactly a staple ingredient in most households."

"She sounds perfect," Lexie said. "When do we meet her?"

Thankfully Jack was saved from having to answer by the arrival of Ron and Diane. Glenn and Sharon got there a few minutes later. Soon Jack's kitchen-cum-family-room was filled with talk and laughter. They poured wine into glasses and set dishes on the long jarrah-wood table surrounded by mismatched wooden chairs all painted a warm deep red. Work clothes had been shed for jeans; everyone had come ready to relax.

Renita's appetizer took longer to prepare than she'd anticipated, but no one minded. They ate her garlicky skewered prawns standing around the kitchen counter, jostling good-naturedly for space, three different conversations going at once.

Jack teased his sisters and joked with his friends, but his thoughts returned over and over to a certain pair of fine gray-green eyes. He was all stocked up, but he found himself thinking about his next trip to the greengrocer. What were the chances he'd run into her again? And could he wait a whole week?

GARLIC AND CHOPPED ONIONS were sizzling in the frying pan. The chicken was on a plate to one side, waiting to be sliced into strips. A bottle of curry paste sat defiantly next to the chicken. Glancing at the clock, Sienna frowned. It was nearly seven-thirty. Glyneth and Rex were late.

"See you later, Mum." Oliver strode through the kitchen, pulling on his jacket. "I'm going to Jason's now."

Sienna tossed the onion and garlic skins into the garbage. "Aren't you staying for dinner?"

"We're going to get a pizza."

Sienna sighed gustily, blowing back the same wayward lock of hair that always came loose and fell over her forehead. Pizza sounded good about now. "Be home by eleven."

"One o'clock." Oliver sniffed the air. "Is something burning?"

With a cry, Sienna whirled to see acrid smoke wafting up from the pan. She flipped the gas off and turned on the fan to carry away the odor of scorched garlic. *"Midnight,"* she said firmly to Oliver. "Call me if you need a ride."

"I'll walk. It's only a few blocks."

"Don't forget your key."

"I won't. See you later."

Sienna grabbed the frying pan and took it to the sink. As she scraped out the burned onion and garlic she heard Oliver's footsteps in the tiled hall, then a moment later the front door shut with a snick.

The phone rang and she left the pan in the sink to reach for the cordless handset on the counter. "Hello?"

"It's me," Glyneth said, sounding harried as she spoke above the sound of traffic. "The car's broken down on the freeway. Rex thinks it's the fuel pump. We've called the auto association, but it's going to be a couple of hours before they get here. I wanted to take a taxi, but Rex won't leave his stupid Jag and I don't have the heart to abandon him. We're not going to make it, Sienna. I'm sorry."

"Oh, hell. I was so looking forward to seeing you guys," Sienna said. "When is Rex going to admit his vintage Jaguar is more trouble than it's worth?"

"God, don't I wish! I hope you didn't go to too much trouble."

Sienna gazed at the haze hanging over the ruin of a kitchen. It wasn't the work and the mess she minded. It was another evening on her own. Glyneth couldn't help that. She straightened her shoulders. "Oh, you know me—I open a packet and heat. I'm just sorry you're stuck out there with car trouble. How about next weekend?"

"We can't. It's Rex's niece's wedding." Glyneth's phone started to crackle with static. "I'm dropping out. I'd better go. I'll call you and we'll catch up soon."

Sienna hung up and rubbed her right temple where a headache was starting. She rummaged in her purse for a bottle of painkillers. Jack Thatcher's card fell out.

She stared at the bold black letters of his name on the white card. Now that her plans had fallen through did she have the guts to take him up on his invitation? Bev had personally vouched for Jack Thatcher, so Sienna wasn't worried that he was some random wacko. And she'd been looking for an opportunity to get out and meet people.

Sienna wasn't interested in pursuing a romantic relationship. She just wanted a distraction and a few friendly faces to fill an otherwise solitary evening. And for all Jack Thatcher's banter she didn't think he was interested, either. He seemed the type to have invited the whole grocery store to dinner.

She'd always been cautious, too controlled to do things on the spur of the moment. Plan ahead had been her motto. That was how she'd gotten through med school and how she'd coped with a demanding workload while being a wife and mother. That hadn't worked so well, she thought wryly. So maybe this was something else in her life she should change. Maybe it was time she trusted her instinct and gave in to impulse.

Before she could talk herself out of it, she wrapped up the food she'd been cooking and put it back in the fridge. A quick shower and a change into her favorite little black dress perked up her spirits. She put her hair up, applied fresh makeup and slipped into her best pair of shoes.

Then she wrote a note for Oliver and left it on the

kitchen counter where he'd see it when he came in. Leaving a light burning over the stove, she slipped out the front door into a fragrant spring evening that suddenly seemed alive with possibility.

CHAPTER THREE

THE DOORBELL RANG just as Jack was sprinkling a generous handful of fresh coriander over the bubbling curry, sending up a pungent, mouthwatering aroma. *Maybe Dad decided to come after all.* He carried the brimming wok to the table, where fat brown candles glowed on either side of a bowl of floating gardenias. Andrea Bocelli's deep tones provided a mellow backdrop to the hum of conversation and laughter.

"Dinner's ready," he announced to his guests. "Go ahead and start. I'll be right back."

As everyone found a place, Renita started dishing out bowls of rice and curry, passing them around the table.

Jack strode down the hall. It would be good if Steve came. He probably wasn't cooking for himself, with Hetty away on her retreat. He swung open the door. "Hi, D—" he began. Then was lost for words.

The woman from the grocery store stood on his doorstep.

Only, it *wasn't* her.

Her gloriously wild hair was tamed into a tightly pinned knot at her nape. She wore a black cocktail dress, high heels and pearls. God forbid he of all people should judge by appearances, but this woman was not the same one he'd invited to dinner.

"My plans fell through..." She trailed off. The nervous smile on her carefully made-up face froze. Uneasiness radiating from her in waves, she presented him with a bottle of red wine. "This isn't very suitable for curry. I didn't stop to get another bottle, since I'm already late—"

"It's okay. I mean, thanks. Come in," he said finally, recovering his manners just this side of rudeness. "It's great you could make it." He stepped back to let her inside. "Er, I never did catch your name."

SIENNA TOOK ONE LOOK at Jack's white T-shirt and faded jeans and cringed. She hadn't missed the bitten-off greeting or his surprise. Whoever he'd been expecting to open the door to, it wasn't her. Dressing up, automatic in her old crowd, had been a huge mistake. How embarrassing. This was what she got for trying to be spontaneous.

"Sienna Maxwell." She licked her lips, tried to take a breath and felt her dress constrict around her rib cage. Hairpins stretched her hair painfully across her skull. She wished she could rip off the pearls and stash them in her purse. Voices, laughter and music came from the other room. There were a *lot* of people here. "I should have called first."

"No, it's fine." He ran a hand through his already rumpled hair. "You're just in time for dinner."

It wasn't fine. She could tell by the tense set of his shoulders as he led the way through the living room and down a short hallway lined with photos. She caught fleeting glimpses of windswept airfields and small airplanes taking off before she was ushered into the dining room.

The candlelit table surrounded by glowing faces was reflected in the darkened floor-to-ceiling windows. Exotic spicy smells filled the air, reminding Sienna she hadn't eaten since lunch, seven hours earlier. Luckily no one would have heard her rumbling stomach over the velvety background music.

Leaning on their elbows, waving wineglasses, Jack's guests were garrulous and jovial. This was exactly the atmosphere she'd wished to find herself in when she'd made the move to Summerside. Except that in the reality of it, she was out of place. An uptight city girl. All eyes turned to regard her curiously. In her designer dress and Manolo Blahnik shoes Sienna couldn't have felt more conspicuous if she'd been wearing her white coat and a stethoscope.

Jack introduced her, then went around the table, firing off the names of his other guests. Standing stiffly, Sienna nodded and smiled, trying to remember who was who. There were more women than men—a major no-no at her friends' dinner parties. She was adding to the uneven gender mix.

Sienna turned to Jack so that her back was to the others and spoke in a low voice. "I'm intruding. I should go."

"No, please." His dark eyes were serious as he touched her elbow. "I'd like it if you stayed."

She searched his face. He *seemed* sincere. "Well… okay."

A plump woman with a dark ponytail—Renita?—jumped up to grab an empty chair and pushed it to the table next to hers. "Sit here," she said, smiling warmly. "I'll get you a plate."

Amid jostling and good-natured squabbles, everyone pulled in their chairs as Sienna edged around the table, brushing against the ferns that framed the windows. Smiling fixedly, she could feel every eye follow her. Finally she sank gratefully into her chair, only to find Jack seated at the end kitty-corner to her, so close their knees touched. Did this not constitute a need for that card table?

"Sorry," she murmured, trying to edge away, but her chair was hard up against the one belonging to the woman with the ponytail...*Renita.* Sienna breathed and forced her shoulders to relax, fighting her urge to run. *Give these people a chance. Give yourself a chance. You've been out of circulation for too long.*

Jack set her bottle of wine in the middle of the table. "Did you want the red or would you like sauvignon blanc? It goes well with curry."

"No wine for me, thanks," Sienna said, putting a hand over her glass. "I'm driving."

It was an excuse. She could easily have one glass of wine without worrying about being impaired. Truth be told, she was nervous. When she was nervous she sometimes drank too much. Doctors weren't supposed to do that. She certainly wasn't about to admit she was afraid of getting tipsy and making a bad impression.

"You won't be driving for hours yet." Jack lifted her wrist away from her glass and poured.

Sienna should have been annoyed at his presumption, but at the touch of his fingertips on her pulse all she could feel was a melting warmth. God, she was an idiot. One of these women had to be Jack's girlfriend.

When she still didn't drink, he leaned closer and whispered in her ear, "Of course you don't have to have wine, but it might help you loosen up."

With Jack's friends openly and unabashedly watching the exchange, she really had no choice. Frankly, she could use a little false courage right about now. Glancing around the table, Sienna lifted her glass. "Cheers."

With her first sip the other guests seemed to relax and conversation resumed. Everyone talked at once, reminding Sienna of those movies she loved about big happy gatherings of family and friends at Christmas or Thanksgiving. A bowl of rice and fragrant chicken curry was passed down the table to her. Condiments and water, cutlery, a linen napkin all came her way in a haphazard fashion.

With the attention moved away from her and Jack, Sienna was able to study her fellow dinner guests. There was Sharon, short, blonde and vivacious, and her husband, Glenn, easygoing and athletic-looking with close-cropped red hair. Ron was stocky with a shaved head that effectively disguised a balding pate. Diane had spiky hennaed hair and a husky voice. That left Jack, Lexie and Renita. Lexie looked to be older and was very pretty. Renita had a warmth about her that was instantly engaging. Both seemed to have an intimate claim on Jack, frequently sending him glances and exchanging teasing comments with him.

Which was his girlfriend?

Not that it mattered one iota to her. She was just curious.

She spooned some of the light coconut broth swimming with chicken. She looked at Jack in amazement. "This is delicious. Better than any meal I've had in a Thai restaurant."

"As good as yours would have been?" he inquired.

"I don't know about that," she demurred, then decided to slip in a mention of Oliver just to get it out of the way. "My son will be forever grateful he didn't have to eat something 'weird.'"

"Your son?"

"Oliver. He's fourteen." She saw the unspoken question in Jack's eyes and steeled herself. "I'm divorced." She glanced away. Every time she spoke those words it felt like an admission of failure.

"I'm a widower."

His low voice touched something inside her and her gaze found his again. "I'm sorry." A flash of something—empathy over life's disappointments, the cruelty of tragedy—connected them for a moment.

Then Jack shrugged, a tiny gesture that carried him from the unalterable past back to the present. He looked around at his guests enjoying themselves and took a sip of wine. "Life goes on."

Sienna breathed out. He was right. She was in a new place, starting afresh. "Yes, it does. Life goes on."

He smiled. She smiled back. Comrades.

Finally she broke the silence with the first thing that came to mind. "So, Jack, what do you do for a living?"

"Nothing much."

Sienna laughed, as no doubt she was supposed to. "No, really, what do you do?"

Before he could answer, Renita interrupted, swiveling on her chair to attract Sienna's attention. "I love your pearls. They're real, aren't they?"

"Yes, they belonged to my grandmother." Sienna ran her fingertips over the long strand self-consciously. "I can see I'm overdressed for the occasion."

"You look amazing," Renita insisted. "Doesn't she, Jack?"

"Please..." Sienna began, feeling heat climb her cheeks.

Jack's eyes rested on her. "You should see her with her hair down."

"Ooh, yes! I'd like to see that," Lexie said from across the table. Her chin rested in one palm as she imperiously waved a wineglass with her other hand. "Pull out those pins."

Sienna laughed uncertainly and focused on her curry. "The Kaffir lime leaves really make a difference." She had no idea what she was talking about, of course. She could still feel Jack's gaze on her.

"Stop it, you guys, you're making her uncomfortable." Sharon came to her rescue. "Sienna, don't mind these three. They tend to pounce on people and gobble them up. It means they like you."

"These three?" For one wild moment she wondered if they were a ménage à trois. Had she stumbled into a hotbed of swinging in the suburbs? Then it dawned on her. The family resemblance. It was in the shape of their eyes and the fullness of the bottom lip. "You're related?"

"Brother and sisters," Ron told her. "They're the evil threesome."

Of course. Sienna glanced from Jack to Lexie to Renita. All three returned her smile. Brother and sisters.

To an only child the bond they shared represented the family love that had always been out of her reach. Her mother was a leader in cancer research and her father was a distinguished heart surgeon, both now working in America at the Mayo Clinic. When she was a child they'd rarely had time for her, while still expecting her to be an overachiever. Sienna had always wanted a sister or a brother. Or both.

She felt something loosen inside her that she didn't understand but also didn't want to examine too closely. Instead, she laughed. Beneath the table she kicked off her shoes.

"WHAT DO *YOU* DO, SIENNA?" Diane asked.

They'd gone around the table, filling Sienna in on themselves. She'd learned that Glenn and Sharon were both primary schoolteachers, Ron was a computer analyst, Diane was a planner for the municipality, Renita worked at the bank and Lexie was a portrait painter.

Lexie chimed in before Sienna could answer. "She could be an artist's model. Look at that oval face and ivory skin. If she let her hair down she'd be Botticelli's Venus. Pure pre-Raphaelite."

"Botticelli's Venus was blonde." Sienna saw Renita topping up her wineglass and started to protest. Then she shrugged. She could always get a taxi.

"Sienna's a pianist," Jack asserted.

She jerked back with a surprised laugh. "I'm not! I can't even play a kazoo."

"A brain surgeon?" Jack's alternative had the whole table in an uproar.

"Warmer," Sienna said coyly. They all stopped laughing. Curious eyes were again trained on her, but now she was comfortable with it. "I'm a doctor. A GP."

"Ahh." Jack's eyes lit with interest.

"I've got a pain in my stomach," Ron called from across the table. "What would cause that, do you think?"

"Overeating, you oaf!" Diane nudged him with her elbow. "What about a pain in the butt? Oh, wait a minute, that's my husband."

Jack cleared his throat and swallowed experimentally, "I think I'm coming down with something. Could it be strep throat?"

Sienna eyed Jack's healthy skin and clear, twinkling eyes skeptically. "I don't do on-the-spot diagnoses. Come into the clinic and I'll give you a thorough examination."

A chorus of oohs from around the table greeted that remark. Sienna felt her blush rise from her neck all the way to the roots of her hair. "You know what I mean!"

"Seriously, are you taking new patients?" Jack asked. "My father's doctor at the clinic retired and Steve needs a checkup."

"Your father must have been seeing my predecessor. I'm taking on most of Dr. Klein's patients. Tell your dad to call the clinic and make an appointment."

"Thanks, I'll pass that on."

Ron got up to clear the empty dishes. Diane rose to help him, waving Sienna down when she started to get up, too. "Relax. We've got it."

Sienna stacked her bowl into Jack's and passed them both to Diane with a smile of thanks. Then she turned to Jack. "You never did say what *you* do for a living."

Jack picked up the wine bottle. "Top you up?"

"I'm good, thanks." This time she put her hand over her glass and kept it there.

"Jack manages his portfolio," Lexie said, giving her brother an affectionate smirk. "Dirty capitalist pig that he is."

Jack shot an answering grin across the table. "Who bails you out when you're behind on your rent?"

"I'm having a show next week at the Manyung Gallery." Lexie sniffed. "Then we'll see who'll be bailing who out."

Sienna smiled at the banter, but she'd noticed that Jack had again avoided answering her question. Both times she'd asked, one of his sisters had jumped in quickly to send the conversation in another direction. "So you're between jobs?"

Jack smiled blandly at her, but a barrier came down over his eyes. "Not quite. I don't work."

For some reason an image of Oliver refusing to go to university flashed into her mind. Sienna shook her head, focusing on the man in front of her. "You must do *something*."

Jack leaned back in his chair, one arm flung over the neighboring chair back, the image of relaxed good humor. Yet tension ran down his shoulder and into his fingers, which were pressed against the red painted wood so hard that the pale pink of his nail bed had turned white.

"He's pretty busy cooking gourmet meals for us all," Renita said.

"And he does a lot of outdoor sports," Lexie added, getting up to finish clearing the table. "Kayaking, cycling, rock climbing, golf."

"He also gives science presentations in schools," Renita said. "Electronics mostly."

So it was him. "Did you recently teach the grade nines at the high school how to build robots out of computer disks?" Sienna asked.

"That's right." Jack looked surprised for a second, then he grinned. "Don't tell me your son is in that class."

"Yes, and he's your biggest fan." She took a sip of water. "What else do you do?"

"I potter around in my shed next door."

"Next door? Do you mean that huge corrugated iron building on the other side of the hedge?"

"This property is a double lot," he explained. "The shed used to house farm machinery before the area became residential. I put in a concrete floor and a small kitchen for making coffee."

"What do you do in there?" Sienna asked. "Do you have a small business?"

"Nothing like that. I was using it to build an ultralight aircraft. Now I mainly fix things," Jack said. "Small stuff. Nothing interesting or important."

"By the way, Jack," Renita interrupted, "you said you'd help me improve my handicap. When are we heading to the links?"

Jack and Renita started talking golf. Renita asked if Sienna played, but she shook her head. Glenn and

Sharon joined in, making a date for the four of them to have a round on Sunday afternoon.

Sienna rose to carry a serving bowl over to the kitchen where Lexie had taken over from Diane in loading the dishwasher. Jack had hobbies, but why was his profession—or lack of it—such a mystery? Digging for more information after that last evasion would be rude, so she said nothing, just rinsed the platters and handed them to Lexie to stack.

"Is there an apron?" Sienna asked. "I'll wash the pots."

"Oh, no, you won't," Lexie said. "We never do them the same night." She tugged Sienna closer to the light over the stove. "Your hair is a lovely jumble of ocher, umber and burnt sienna. Rather appropriate, that last one." Her small paint-stained hands hovered over Sienna's head. "I've just *got* to see you with your hair down. Do you mind?" Without waiting for permission, she started pulling out the hairpins that held Sienna's up-do in place.

Sienna jerked back. Some of her long fiery hair sprang free and fell in a heavy coil down her neck.

"Lexie!" Jack exclaimed as he came into the kitchen to put on the kettle for coffee. "What have I told you about manhandling people?" He added a warning to Sienna. "Next she'll be feeling the shape of your skull."

"She doesn't mind. Do you, Sienna?" A pin fell from Lexie's fingers and clattered onto the floor. "I'm looking for a sitter for the Archibald Prize portrait contest," she explained. "You'd be perfect."

"I..." Sienna glanced around. No one else was paying

any attention, intent on the cake Diane had brought. Apparently among this group of friends, such familiar behavior, even to a newcomer, wasn't out of the ordinary.

Lexie took out the last of the pins and Sienna's hair sprang loose in a cascade of long curls around her face and down her back. "Wow."

"To tell you the truth, this is a relief." Sienna pushed her hands through her hair to massage her scalp.

Jack, attempting to plug the kettle in, jabbed at the outlet blindly as he stared at her. He might well be surprised, she thought. When he'd seen her earlier her hair had been tied back in a ponytail.

Lexie enthusiastically plunged her fingers straight into the springy mass. "It's so thick and silky. Jack, feel it."

"No," Sienna started to protest, embarrassed, but Jack already had his fingers in her hair.

"Nice." His eyes were on hers, and his thumb made contact with the tender skin behind her ear. He stroked just once, lightly. "Very nice."

Her breath jammed in her lungs. She couldn't look away from his gaze. If Lexie hadn't been standing right there, she would have half expected him to kiss her.

"How's that coffee coming?" Glenn called. "Sharon's mum is minding the kids and she swears she turns into a pumpkin at midnight."

"Coming right up." Jack removed his hand, squeezed her shoulder and went to the cupboard for cups.

Sienna let her breath out. Now she was aware of her heart pounding. She went back to the table to find that everyone had shifted places and broken into smaller groups to chat. At Diane's encouraging smile she dropped into an empty chair between her and Sharon and the pair included her in their conversation about gardening. Discussing new varieties of drought-tolerant plants was a relief after the charged atmosphere in the kitchen.

Gradually Sienna relaxed again. But every time she glanced up she caught Jack's eye. He was sitting across from her now. She could swear he was keeping one ear open to her conversation, just as she was with his talk with Ron and Glenn about the marine life he'd seen while diving on the Great Barrier Reef.

His recent travels explained why she'd never run into him in the village until today. He certainly seemed to have a lot of time on his hands. She told herself it shouldn't bother her that he didn't work, but it did. Coming from a long line of high achievers, she had a strong work ethic deeply ingrained in her. Jack was only in his mid to late thirties, healthy, intelligent, not handicapped in any way. There must be more to the story than met the eye. At least, she hoped so.

SHORTLY AFTER MIDNIGHT Jack walked Renita to where she'd parked her BMW a couple of doors down. The night was balmy with the scent of jasmine drifting on the light breeze. A half-moon, very bright in the clear sky, hung above the treetops. Everyone but Sienna had already left. She was in the house, calling a taxi. He hoped to have a few minutes with her before the cab came.

"I'll pick you up for golf tomorrow at one-thirty," he said to Renita as she unlocked her door. "Maybe you can look over the prospectus for that investment company I'm interested in and tell me what you think."

"Sure thing. Great dinner tonight, as usual." Renita hugged him and slid into the driver's seat. She rolled down the window and Jack leaned down. "She's nice."

"She is," Jack agreed. There was no doubt who they were talking about. "I'm not sure she approves of me."

"You're too sensitive, Jack."

"She's a doctor. You know what they're like. Life revolves around work."

"Yes, she's a doctor. That's a *good* thing." Renita turned the key in the ignition and the motor purred to life. She put the car in gear. "Maybe she'll heal you."

Jack stepped back from the curb as Renita drove off. He watched the red taillights disappear around the corner, then he turned and walked back to the house. He was sure Sienna was highly competent with diseases of the body; possibly she even had knowledge of illnesses of the mind. But his sickness was in his soul.

While he craved company, he shunned true intimacy. He knew that about himself and accepted it with a clear-eyed fatalism. Sure, the love of the right woman might heal him. But what if it didn't? He was capable of inflicting damage without wanting to, without even being aware he was doing so. His one disastrous attempt at a relationship after Leanne had shown him that.

Anyway, he had an idea Sienna had a wound or two of her own. If they could be *friends,* maybe they could heal each other.

He stepped onto the path to his door and stopped. She was standing beneath the porch light, her hair a burnished mantle flowing over her shoulders. Her feet were bare. Her shoes and purse dangled from her fingers. In the space of a few hours she'd come all undone. It was a sexy look.

Friendship was a beautiful thing, but he felt a stab of regret for the possibilities he was denying himself.

"The taxi's on its way," she said as he climbed the steps to her. She shifted her shoes to her other hand. Glanced up and down the street. She was back to being nervous. "It's still warm."

Jack leaned against the pillar supporting the veranda roof. "I'm glad you were able to come tonight after all."

She glanced at her watch. "I wonder where that taxi is."

"It's only a little after twelve."

"Oliver didn't know I was going out. I left a note, but I've never been gone when he's come home before." As if realizing what this told him about her social life, she shrugged and gave him a sheepish grin. "I don't get out much since my divorce."

"Was it messy?" he asked, sympathetic.

"No more than most, I suppose." Her mouth tightened as she glanced away. "Anthony and I talk. Oliver keeps us amicable."

Why did he get the impression that despite her casual manner, she was hurting inside? "Are you sure you wouldn't like to join us for golf tomorrow?"

"I'd only slow you down. I'm guessing you're pretty good, with all the free time you have to spend on sports." She blushed and tugged on a strand of hair. "Sorry. I didn't mean that as a dig."

Maybe not consciously, Jack thought, but he decided not to take offense. Instead, he said mildly, "We don't play competitively. Renita's not much more than a novice."

"Thanks, but it's the one day of the week I can spend time with Oliver. And I need to make sure he does his homework."

"Is he a good student?"

"He could be a whole lot better," she admitted. "He's smart, but he doesn't apply himself."

"Fourteen is a tough age for school. I hated it."

Sienna's gaze flicked to his clearly expensive house and back to him. "You really don't work at anything?"

"Life's short," he said flippantly. "I live for pleasure."

Suspicion clouded her eyes. "Then how do you get money?"

"I'm not a drug dealer. Nothing illegal is going on."

"But you must have worked at some time in the past."

"The past is a foreign country. I lost my passport."

"Mr. Mysterious, eh?" She leaned on the porch railing, studying him. "Are you really content with just hobbies?"

He sensed she wanted to like him. He wasn't being egotistical to think that. And he was attracted to her. Yet it was clear she couldn't help judging him. Self-indulgent. Lazy. Hedonistic. He could almost hear the pronouncements flowing through her mind. Those qualities weren't what she, a doctor, stood for.

"I'm not a bad person," he said, attempting to make

a joke of it. "In fact, you and I operate by the same code—'First, do no harm.'"

"You don't do harm by having a job."

"I had a job once. I ran a light-aircraft charter. I was a pilot. I also built and repaired engines and navigational systems." He gave her a twisted smile. "A 'Jack' of all trades, you could say."

"That sounds amazing," she said. "Why did you stop?"

He shrugged. "I got tired of it."

"Really?" she said, dubious. "Will you ever go back to it?"

"No. Never." It *had* been a great job, one he loved. But he'd screwed up big-time. Leanne had paid the price. "Look, it's best not to have expectations of me. I don't like to disappoint."

"Are you warning me off?" Sienna asked.

"No, that's not it. Not exactly." But he suspected she had a fairly rigid definition of success and he didn't meet the criteria.

"It's okay." Her glance went past his shoulder. "There's the taxi." She bent to slip her shoes back on. From somewhere she found a hair tie and tamed the mass of auburn curls into a ponytail.

"Thanks so much for a wonderful evening, Jack. The food was marvelous. Your friends are lovely." She was smiling as she circled around him, one foot on the next step down. "I really enjoyed myself."

"Come again, anytime."

"Love to." Her tone was light.

The taxi's headlights were behind her, so he couldn't

see her expression. Did she mean it, or were her cool gray-green eyes sending another message entirely?

In a way he supposed he *had* been warning her off. He'd built a comfortable life, one he could live with. His friends understood him—well, as much as anyone could understand someone who didn't spill his guts at the drop of a hat—and enjoyed him for who he was.

The problem with women was they always thought they could change you. He was quite happy being himself, thank you very much. He didn't want anyone, not even a redheaded Venus, rocking his carefully balanced boat.

CHAPTER FOUR

SIENNA APPLIED a sizzling drop of liquid nitrogen to the plantar wart on the sole of her forty-three-year-old female patient's right foot. "This shouldn't hurt..."

Penelope Brown reclined on the examining table with her pant leg rolled up over her calf. Her long dark bangs fell over eyes scrunched tightly shut. "Will this get rid of it? I'm on my feet for long hours in the classroom."

"The wart will turn black and die within a few days. If it doesn't, or if it gets hot and swollen, come back and see me." Sienna returned the applicator to the stainless steel container and closed the lid on the clouds of vapor. "Keep your feet clean and dry," she added, taping a bandage over the wart. "Don't go barefoot in public swimming pools or showers."

"Okay." Penelope pushed herself to a sitting position and put her stocking back on. She slid off the examining table and reached for her purse.

When Sienna handed her an information sheet on foot hygiene, Penelope passed her a notice in return. "If you feel like a fun evening for a good cause, come to our Trivia Night."

"Is this to raise funds for the high school?" Sienna asked, scanning the notice. "My son, Oliver, hasn't brought home any information about this."

"It's in the school newsletter going out today. The

sporting facilities need upgrading, but the budget has blown out for this year," Penelope said. "We're trying to encourage the kids to get active instead of sitting in front of the computer all day."

"That *is* a good cause. I'll be there."

"Oh, and we're looking for items to raffle off if you've got anything to donate."

"A free flu vaccination or tonsillectomy?" Sienna joked. "I'll see what I can come up with."

"I'd better scoot," Penelope said, chuckling. "Thanks a lot." She slipped on her shoes and went out the door, closing it behind her.

Sienna tacked the Trivia Night notice to the cork-board beside her desk and went out to greet her next patient, Steve Thatcher. Jack hadn't said anything overt the other evening, but Sienna sensed he was worried about his dad.

In the waiting room, a teenage girl in a school uniform thumbed through a fashion magazine. A harried mother tried to stop her toddler from pulling all the magazines off the coffee table. The portly older man with gray hair and glasses had to be Steve.

In a calm, cheerful voice, Sienna said, "Mr. Thatcher? Come with me, please."

Sienna led the way to her office and waited outside the door while Steve slowly followed. She used the time to make a preliminary medical assessment. His file stated he was sixty-three, although he moved more slowly than some men a decade older. Steve's arms and legs were thin, but his bloated barrel-shaped torso set alarm bells ringing. She already had a suspicion what might be wrong with him.

Sienna gestured for him to take a seat. Balancing on the Swiss exercise ball that served as her desk chair, she brought up his details on the computer.

"I met your son," she said as she typed in the date. To her discomfort her cheeks grew warm. It was a reasonable comment under the circumstances, but she was starting to feel like a schoolgirl who wanted to repeat the name of the guy she had a crush on to everyone she met.

"Whole damn town knows Jack," Steve said gruffly but with a hint of pride.

"Oh, and I met Renita and Lexie, too," she added belatedly. Sienna swiveled to face him, taking in his pale skin and pouchy brown eyes behind the old-fashioned steel-framed glasses. "What can I do for you, Mr. Thatcher?"

"I'm here for a checkup. The missus made me come."

"How are you feeling?" Sienna asked, taking his wrist to check his pulse. A bit fast.

"Well, not that good. I'm tired all the time even though I don't do what you'd call exercise." Steve rubbed a sausage-fingered hand over his stubbly gray jaw. "Sometimes my feet go all tingly. Hurts to walk, like."

"Hop up on the exam table. Undo the top buttons of your shirt so I can check your heart." Sienna got up and nudged her exercise ball under the desk. Plugging her stethoscope into her ears, she slipped the chest piece inside Steve's shirt and pressed it against his chest. His heartbeat was also erratic, but that could be due to any one of several things. "Are you hungry a lot? Excessively thirsty?"

"Yes." He seemed surprised she'd know. "I'm guzzling water day and night. Must be why I'm always going to the toilet. Do you think it could be my prostate?"

"It's possible, but there could be other reasons." Sienna moved the stethoscope to the center of his chest. "Cough for me." Steve forced air out in a bark, repeating it as she moved the stethoscope around. "Your lungs are fine. Do you have a sweet tooth, Mr. Thatcher?"

"Afraid so." Steve grinned, somewhat shamefaced. "My wife loves to bake—cookies, cakes, pies. She gives me heck, but her cakes are that good." His smile faded and a troubled frown deepened the creases on his forehead. "She *used* to bake, that is, when we were living on the farm. Now that we're retired she's into yoga or Eastern mysticism or some such rubbish. She's never home."

"So you're not eating sweets now?" Sienna asked, letting the stethoscope dangle around her neck.

"Oh, yeah, I still do. She made brownies the other day. First time in ages." He rubbed a hand through his sparse gray hair. "But usually I make do with store-bought cakes. They aren't as good, but I eat them anyway."

Sienna sensed that despite Steve Thatcher's gruff demeanor he was feeling lost and lonely. If so, he wouldn't be the first person to turn to food for comfort. Especially if he had too much time on his hands. "Do you have hobbies?"

"I've never had time for hobbies. Wouldn't know where to start now."

Sienna strapped the blood pressure cuff to his upper arm. "Have you thought about joining a seniors' activity group?"

"I'm not gonna knit lace doilies," Steve grumbled.

"Gardening?" she asked, pumping up the cuff.

"Too much work," Steve said, shaking his head. "I spent my whole life running a dairy farm. I've earned a rest."

"Some people find it therapeutic to grow their own flowers and vegetables," Sienna suggested. "You can meet people through gardening clubs—"

"Hell, no! Pardon my language," Steve replied. "Hetty used to belong to a gardening club. You wouldn't believe the backbiting that went on. Whose roses smell the sweetest, whose compost don't stink."

"Okay, no gardening," Sienna said, chuckling as she slowly allowed the pressure to bleed off. "At least you've got family. Do you have grandchildren? I know Jack doesn't, but Renita and Lexie didn't mention if they had children."

"None of them are married or have children," Steve replied. "I see the kids a fair bit, but they all have busy lives. Smedley's 'bout the only one who's got time for me."

"Smedley?"

"My Jack Russell terrier." Steve's face brightened. "He's just a pup, but he's a little ripper."

"Dogs are wonderful companions." Sienna checked the digital readout. "Your blood pressure's high. When did you last have your sugar levels tested?"

Steve shrugged, his expression blank. "Can't say as I've ever had that done."

Sienna stripped the cuff off his arm and stepped back. "You can do up your shirt and get down now." Dropping back onto her ball, she tapped at the computer keys. "I'm ordering some blood tests. It's possible you have type 2 diabetes. We won't know for certain until I see the results."

"Diabetes? That can't be." Agitated, he rubbed his hands on his thighs, pushing his brown pants back and forth. "Our neighbor's kid has diabetes. Poor mite is real sickly. Gets jabbed with needles day and night."

"He most likely has type 1 diabetes. There's no need for you to be alarmed," Sienna assured him. "Untreated, type 2 can have serious consequences but it's a manageable condition. A person doesn't necessarily need to take insulin. There are other medications, and diet and exercise can help a lot. First we need to find out if you have it."

"I can't have diabetes," Steve repeated stubbornly. "I've always been as healthy as a horse. It's probably just a touch of flu."

"We'll see." The lab request printed out and she ripped it from the machine. "Take this to the pathology lab next door first thing Monday morning. The full instructions are on this sheet. Don't eat or drink anything for at least twelve hours beforehand. I recommend you cut back on the sweets until we find out the results."

Sienna studied Steve's downcast face as he scanned the instruction sheet. He wasn't her only patient who had trouble adjusting to retirement. Men especially, it seemed, often had no idea what to do with themselves once they stopped working. In Steve's case, add a move to a new community and a wife whose interests differed from his. She wouldn't be surprised if Steve was suffering from mild depression as well as diabetes.

"Would you be interested in joining a Men's Shed?" she asked, suddenly recalling a recent magazine article extolling the virtues of the not-for-profit organization. Men's Sheds tackled men's physical and emotional health issues by providing them with a place to go to socialize and engage in productive activities.

"I've heard of them." Steve looked up with a faint gleam of interest. "Is there a Men's Shed in Summerside?"

"I'll find out. Hang on just a tick." Sienna reached for the phone and dialed her local fount of knowledge. "Bev, do you know where the closest Men's Shed is? Okay, thanks." She hung up and turned to Steve. "Rosebud. That's only what, half an hour down the highway?"

"We sold the second car when we moved to Summerside and the missus is always off somewhere in the one we've got left. Anyway, my eyesight isn't the greatest lately."

"Diabetes can affect your vision. You should get your eyes checked, too."

He blinked at her, unwavering and stolid. "I don't have diabetes."

"Well, hopefully not. But we need to find out."

"You go by that doctor-patient confidentiality thing don't you, Doc?" Steve asked. "You won't tell Jack about this."

"I don't know your son that well. But why don't you want him to know? Your family could be a support."

"No," he said firmly as he rose and went to the door. "I don't want anyone fussing over me."

Or was it that he didn't want anyone bugging him to eat right and exercise? *Jack could run a Men's Shed.* The thought leaped into Sienna's mind as she was seeing Steve out. *He has the space, the time, the personality and the practical skills.*

The idea grew on her over the course of the afternoon. She found a few minutes to look up Men's Sheds on the Internet and make a phone call to the national association. The more she found out, the more excited she became about the possibilities, not just for Steve, but all the men in the community with too much time on their hands.

Including Jack. Running a Men's Shed might be just what he needed to give him renewed purpose. Despite his happy-go-lucky attitude, she sensed an undercurrent of restlessness, even dissatisfaction. To her, it seemed a perfect fit.

She started to reach for the phone book, then changed her mind. She would go over to his place after work. That way he wouldn't find it as easy to say no. True, he'd made it clear he had no ambition. But surely he would consider taking on the Men's Shed if it meant helping his father.

"OLIVER!" SHE CALLED, coming through her front door later that afternoon. "Are you home?"

"In the kitchen." He shambled into view with a sandwich in hand. Taking a big bite, he mumbled around the food, "What's up?"

"Don't talk with your mouth full." Sienna dropped her purse and folder of papers on the counter to get herself a drink of water. "I have to go see Jack Thatcher about something. I won't be long."

"Okay," Oliver said without much interest. Then he glanced up, eyes widening. "Hang on. I think Jack Thatcher is the guy who gave the robotics presentation to my class."

"That's right. I need to speak to him about starting a Men's Shed in Summerside."

"Can I come? I want him to show me how to install a gear in my robot so it'll go in reverse."

"I don't know about that," she said. "He might not want to be bothered at home with school stuff."

"He won't mind, honest," Oliver said. "He told the class we could come around to his place anytime and he'd answer any questions or help us with projects."

"Speaking of projects, how was school today?"

"Crappy, as usual."

"Define crappy."

"Mum, we're wasting time!"

"Okay, let's go. But this conversation isn't over."

JACK LAY IN BED, arms outstretched, staring at the ceiling, trying to think of a reason he should get up. Most days he could cope, even enjoy life. But today was Leanne's birthday. She would have been thirty-three. Jack would have baked her a cake. There might have been a little boy or girl to help her blow the candles out on her birthday cake.

He had no tears left. That at least would have meant he felt something. Instead, an all-pervading numbness spread from his heart outward, paralyzing him. He wasn't sure he could move if he tried. It felt like work to turn his head to glance at the clock. Ten-thirty.

He thought about the week ahead and wondered how he would fill it. When he described his life to others, he made it sound jam-packed, but it wasn't, not really. Evenings, when his friends were available to hang out, he could handle, but too often the days stretched without incident, empty squares on the calendar.

A warm tongue lapped at his fingers dangling over the side of the bed. Bogie.

Jack roused himself. "Hey, buddy. Do you want to go out?"

He let the dog out, forced himself to eat breakfast even though he had no appetite. An hour later he was walking up the gravel driveway breathing in the warm spring air scented by the towering pines. His big plan for the day was to come up with a prototype of a more advanced robot high-school students might enjoy building.

He hoped the activity would drive Sienna out of his thoughts. She'd deflated his ego. Without any false modesty it had been a while since a woman hadn't succumbed to the Jack Thatcher charm. Well, so what? He didn't need a judgmental female in his life.

He unlocked the shed and pulled back the creaking corrugated iron door. His hand found the light switch and he illuminated the cavernous shed. To the immediate left was a long workbench, tools neatly hung from a board on the wall. The far left wall was covered in open shelving crammed with spare parts for just about anything electronic or mechanical.

To the right were a kitchenette and a sitting area

with a battered couch, an area rug and a wood-burning heater. At the back of the shed was a half-finished ultra-light aircraft, a reminder of everything he'd abandoned. The three-wheeled chassis and cockpit were intact, but the struts and the wings were stacked behind it on the floor. After the crash he hadn't been able to complete the machine, but he couldn't quite bring himself to get rid of it, either. Sort of like the GPS he'd invented.

Later that afternoon, Jack was sawing a sheet of transparent yellow resin into strips he could file down for the body and legs of a robot dog when he heard the knock at the open door. He glanced over his shoulder and did a double take. "Come in."

Sienna's bright hair was tied back, but tendrils escaped and curled around her high cheekbones. Her slim square shoulders and narrow waist were defined by a tailored white blouse and a dark pencil skirt. He shouldn't be interested. He *wasn't* interested. But despite what his head said, his heart beat a jig.

With her was a gangly teenager he recognized from a recent school presentation. Jack remembered the boy because he'd asked a lot of questions and he seemed bright. Ah, yes, he was carrying the computer-disk robot Jack had shown the Year 9 class how to build.

"Hi." Sienna approached slowly, glancing around. "This is Oliver, my son. He's been raving about your visit to his science class."

"I didn't *rave,*" Oliver muttered. His face turned bright red but he gave Jack an awkward wave. "Hey."

"Nice to see you again, Oliver." Giving him some space to recover his composure, Jack turned to Sienna. "To what do I owe the pleasure?"

"Your father was in to see me today," she began.

"How is he?" Jack said. "Is there anything wrong?"

Sienna's mouth shut abruptly. After a moment's hesitation she said, "He's getting some blood tests done—nothing unusual for a man of his age. The reason I mentioned him is that he represents a more general problem many men in the community face."

She started spreading printouts from the internet over his bench. Oliver drifted toward the ultralight. "Don't touch anything, Olly," she warned, clearly one of those mothers with eyes in the back of her head.

"He can't hurt anything." Jack looked over her shoulder at the brochures and breathed in the smell of her hair. The print blurred. Pineapple. He loved pineapple.

"The government provides start-up funding, but once the shed is running it's like a small business. It needs a source of income to be self-sustaining."

She was so eager to get her message across, her words tumbled out. "You can make toys for a child-care center or benches for the park. The projects you choose depend on what your group is skilled at. The main thing is it's a place for men like your dad to connect and engage in productive activities." She stopped for breath and looked at him, her eyes shining. "What do you think?"

"I know about Men's Sheds," Jack said. "But what do they have to do with me?"

"I'm talking about you starting up a Men's Shed, *here.*" She glanced around at the interior, as big as three double garages. "You can get funding to upgrade the facilities if necessary. I've even thought of a first project for your group—making toys to raffle off at the high school's Trivia Night. They're raising funds for better sporting facilities. You would appreciate that. As the leader you get a salary—"

"Whoa! Stop right there." Jack put his hands up to halt the flow of what she clearly thought was a brilliant idea. "I'm not leading anything."

"But you're perfect for the job." Sienna blinked, bewildered. "You've got the skills, the time—"

"That's *my* time," Jack said, cutting her off again. "To pursue *my* interests." Jeez, but he sounded selfish when he put it that way. And considering how hard he'd found it to get out of bed this morning, he probably ought to do it. But he just couldn't. Softening his tone, he added, "I've never been good at sticking to someone else's schedule. That's why I used to have my own business."

Sienna's face cleared. "From what the head of the Men's Shed Association told me, each shed sets their own agenda—"

"You already talked to the head of the association? I hope you didn't mention my name."

Guilt all over her face, she glanced away. Then she turned to him again, her small, pointed jaw determined. "I just wanted to have all the facts for when I talked to you. Nothing's carved in stone."

"Good, because it's not going to happen. At least not in my shed, run by me." He started to shift her papers off his robot parts.

"Your father is bored and lonely. He's—" Again she stopped abruptly. "He needs an active interest. There are a lot of men like him out there."

"Look, I'm more than happy for Dad or Oliver or anyone to come and have a cup of coffee or potter with my tools. But I don't want to be tied to a schedule or held accountable by community organizations."

"You might—"

"No, I won't."

"Let me finish!"

He crossed his arms and fixed her with a stare.

"You might *enjoy* it. You might get something out of it yourself." Barely audible, she added, "A purpose in life."

He'd hoped she might be different. But no, she was just another do-gooder bent on saving him from himself. Something she seemed to need more than he did. So what if he had a bad day once in a while? "I *have* a purpose to my life. To get as much pleasure out of it as I possibly can."

"I refuse to believe you're that…hedonistic," she said, shaking her head.

"Don't go thinking there's some deep side to me," he snapped. "I'm totally out for myself."

"I know that's not true," she said. "You got Olly and his classmates interested in electronics. I happen to know you didn't get paid for that."

Jack waved that off. "Money isn't an issue. I don't like being responsible for others."

"Okay." She held her hands up, surrendering. "I just thought you might enjoy it. I apologize for putting you on the spot."

"Don't worry about it. I don't have a problem saying no."

She walked back to the workbench and started stacking her brochures and papers, tapping them down into alignment. "Olly wanted to ask you something."

Jack walked over to the boy, who was peering into the cockpit of the ultralight.

"Did you build this?" Oliver asked, awestruck.

"I'm in the process of it." Not wanting to explain why three years had passed since he'd done a lick of work on it, Jack gestured to the CD Oliver was holding. "How's your robot working?"

"I'd like to make it go in reverse. Can you show me how?"

"I've got a gizmo that should do the trick. Come with me." Jack led the way to a spot farther down the workbench from where Sienna waited. He searched through a large plastic container whose many compartments held wheels, gears, levers, cogs and miscellaneous parts for robotic applications. Finally he found what he was looking for.

"Take off the original motor and we'll install this one," he told Oliver. "It's got gears and it's bigger, so you'll be able to move this baby faster. See this slide switch? You push it back to put it in reverse."

Oliver unwired the gearbox from the disk, his blond head bent over the task. "Would wheels work on this instead of the rubber legs?"

"Sure. If you've got any old toy cars lying around, pull them off and attach them. Just make sure they're on an axle so they'll spin freely." Jack handed the new gearbox to Oliver. "You put it on."

Oliver maneuvered the parts into position, his face turning red from being watched.

"That's right," Jack said. "You've got it."

"Does this wire go here?" Olly looked to Jack for confirmation.

Jack nodded. “Make sure you get a tight contact.”

Oliver got the robot moving forward, then flipped the switch into reverse. The disk tottered backward. He shot Jack a wide grin. “I did it!”

“Excellent work.” Jack clapped a hand on his shoulder.

Oliver pushed the switch again, sending the robot forward. Leaving him to play with it, Jack crossed the few steps to Sienna. “He’s quick on the uptake, more so than most of the kids in his class.”

“He’s a smart boy,” Sienna said, watching her son.

Jack leaned against the wooden bench. He didn’t know why he should care what she thought, but something made him ask, “Are you annoyed because I won’t fall in with your Men’s Shed plans?”

“Look, I’ll admit I’m disappointed,” she added. “I thought my idea would be perfect for you, your father and the community at large and I really wanted it to work. But I’ll get over it.” Her sigh was so slight it was barely perceptible. Then she glanced at her watch and called to her son. “Olly, are you finished?”

“In a minute.” He reversed the robot and watched it totter back across the bench.

“Now, Olly.”

“Okay, okay.” Oliver picked up his robot, his eyes bright. “This is so cool,” he said to Jack. “Thanks.”

“Any time. Drop by after school and I’ll show you some more stuff.” He raised an eyebrow at Sienna. “If it’s okay with your mother, that is.”

“As long as it doesn’t interfere with his schoolwork,” she said. “Again, I’m sorry I was so pushy earlier. Thank you for being so generous with your time.”

Her gratitude had the effect of making him feel small. Which irritated him. Who was she to come in here and expect him to follow her whims?

Then as she walked out the door Jack's gaze dropped to her legs. A shaft of sunlight illuminated a small shell tattooed on her shapely ankle.

Damn, but he was in trouble.

CHAPTER FIVE

"SIENNA." BEV POKED her head into the staff room where Sienna, between patients, leaned against the counter eating a sandwich. "Renita Thatcher is here."

"Coming." Sienna swallowed the last bite of turkey and lettuce and washed it down with coffee. She'd been a bit surprised to see Renita's name on her list today until Bev told her that Renita usually saw Phillip Boucher, who was on holiday.

Jack's younger sister's taupe suit fit snugly over her ample bust and hips. It was a far cry from the casual dress Sienna had seen on her last Saturday.

Smiling, she said, "Renita? Would you like to come in now?" She led the way back down the hall.

"Have a seat." Sienna gestured to the chair next to her desk and sank onto her exercise ball. "How've you been?"

"I think I have a sinus infection." Renita's voice was clogged and nasal. She pressed her fingers to her forehead. "Thanks for seeing me. Is it okay that I came to you, I mean since we're friends?"

"If you're comfortable with it, I'm fine." Sienna warmed inside at Renita considering her a friend so quickly. She rose and went to the cabinet for her otoscope. "Are your sinuses hurting?"

Renita nodded. "It started Sunday morning. I thought

at first it was just a cold, but the pain is bad all around my eyes and nose. I can hardly breathe."

Sienna pulled up a chair, pushed Renita's hair back and inserted the instrument to examine her eardrum. It was red and swollen. "Any fever? Yellow or green nasal discharge?"

"Yes to fever and yellow discharge."

Sienna took routine blood pressure and heart rate measurements and tapped her observations into her computer. "I'll give you a prescription for antibiotics. Take an antihistamine as well to dry it up. You should start to feel better in a few days."

"Jack mentioned you asked him to start up a Men's Shed."

Ah. She'd wondered if he would mention it to his sister. "Has he changed his mind?"

"No. May I?" Renita reached for a tissue from the box on Sienna's desk and blew her nose. "I just hope you don't think badly of him for refusing."

The printer started to spit out the prescription. "It's not up to me to tell him what to do. He's obviously got his life figured out."

"He went through a really rough time after his wife, Leanne, died. He hasn't gotten over it. He doesn't like talking about it."

"I'm very sorry," Sienna said quietly. "The Men's Shed might take his mind off his loss."

"Jack's fine." Renita shrugged, balling her tissue in her fist.

Sienna hesitated. "Do you really believe that?" When Renita glanced away, she couldn't help pursuing the point. "I don't mean to be judgmental, but I can't imagine not having a purpose in life. The philosophy of living purely for today makes no sense."

Renita offered her a sad smile. "When your past has been wiped out and you can't bear the thought of the future, the present is all you have."

Sienna was silenced momentarily at the thought of Jack's grief. Then she said, "You just have to pick yourself up and keep going."

"That's what he's doing," Renita replied.

Sienna bit her lip. She should just butt out. This was not professional. Her mother always told her to remember she was a doctor, not a friend or a therapist or a relative. Jack wasn't even her patient. "Look, I'm sorry. This is none of my business. Forget I said anything."

Renita twisted the sodden tissue. "This might be premature, but Lexie and I were hoping that you and he might get together..."

That such a gorgeous man came with two cool sisters was a bonus. But in spite of her strong attraction to Jack she knew that in the long term she couldn't be happy with anyone so aimless.

Your standards are too high for ordinary mortals to live up to. Anthony had said that the night she'd confronted him about his affair with Erica. It had stung. Until she remembered that Anthony was defending his weakness and deceit. High standards were *good.*

"Jack and I aren't right for each other, I'm afraid." Sienna rose and handed Renita the prescription. "If you're not starting to feel better in a few days, come see me again."

SMEDLEY RACED INTO THE SHED, darted over to Jack for a quick sniff, then dashed to Bogie, who was crashed out on the floor by the couch. Bogie lifted his shaggy golden head as Smedley bounced twice on all four legs, a clear invitation to play.

"Hey, Dad," Jack said, seeing Steve's bulky form outlined in the bright light of the doorway. "Come on in."

"I brought some cinnamon buns." Steve took the bag to the kitchen. "I'll put coffee on."

"Go ahead." Jack's fingers were greasy from the lawn mower engine he was overhauling for his father. He'd removed the handle and had the base overturned on the benchtop. "I've almost got this finished."

"No rush." Steve plugged in the kettle. "Take a break."

Jack ignored the suggestion. Although Sienna's attitude toward his lifestyle rankled, since her visit he'd decided to tackle a few projects he'd been putting off. When he looked back over the past year he hadn't accomplished half of what he had in the first two years after his "early retirement." Once he'd recovered from his injuries and got his strength back he'd done heaps of things—painted his entire house and Lexie's, landscaped Renita's garden, organized the sale of his parents' farm and machinery, helped a friend at his winery…and much more.

This year, not so much. Parkinson's Law, "work expands to fill the time allotted," seemed to hold true for him. Never mind. Once he got these few tasks out of the way he'd go back to enjoying life.

Steve got himself a cinnamon bun and wandered over to the ultralight, a natural draw for everyone, it seemed. "It's been a while since you've flown."

Three years, two months and one week. Of course, Steve didn't mean the ultralight—that was just a toy—but a real plane like the Cessna 172 Jack used to charter out. He fitted the rotary blade to the motor. "Your lawn must be a mile high now."

"I should get a sheep. It'd be easier." Steve wiggled the joystick. "Seems a shame you gave it all up. Don't you miss it?"

Jack tightened the screws on the blade, hiding the sharp ache tugging at his insides. Yeah, he missed flying. He missed the surge of power at liftoff and the weightless feeling that followed. He missed the buffeting wind and the exhilaration of soaring through the wide-open sky. He missed the quiet satisfaction of a safe landing and a hot cup of coffee afterward. Keeping the ultralight in the shed was a peculiar form of self-torture. Flying had once been his greatest joy.

"I've got my hands full with this and that." He turned the lawn mower over and wiped it down with a rag. Glancing up, he saw Steve wince and hold his stomach. "What's wrong? Are you sick?"

Steve grimaced again. "I think the meat pie I had for dinner last night was a bit dodgy."

"Jeez, Dad, what are you doing eating meat pies that have gone off? Come over to my place for dinner."

"Your meals are too spicy for my poor stomach." He lumbered over to the couch and sat down heavily.

"So I'll make you roast lamb. When's Mum coming home?"

"Dunno," Steve said with a gloomy scowl. "I thought when we retired we'd travel around the country together. But no, she'd rather go on an inner journey by herself."

"She's found something that makes her happy." Jack defended his mother. Even so, he felt sorry for his father, who'd been left behind.

"We should never have sold the farm," Steve complained, rubbing a hand across his thigh. "She wouldn't have gotten all enlightened and I would have chores to do."

Jack set about reattaching the handle to the base of the lawn mower. "You should make some friends in Summerside," he said, fitting a bolt. "Join the lawn bowling club."

"You sound like the doctor," Steve grumbled. "Killing time, I call those sorts of activities. Give me something worth doing and I'd do it."

A twinge of guilt made Jack turn the wrench too hard. He swore as he stripped the bolt. "Your house doesn't keep you busy?"

"I've fixed every bloody thing that needs fixing, some twice."

Jack worked in silence a moment. He hated to admit it, but Sienna was right—his dad needed something. "Do you remember that wooden rocking horse you made for me when I was small? And the dollhouses you built for Lexie and Renita?"

"'Course." Steve helped himself to another cinnamon bun.

"That sugary stuff will kill you," Jack warned.

"Once in a while doesn't hurt." Steve licked the icing off his fingers.

"You still got the patterns?"

"They must be somewhere in the boxes I stored in the garage," Steve said. "Why?"

"Just thinking. Would you go to a Men's Shed if one was available?"

"Have you been talking to that doctor, Sienna?" Agitated, Steve put down his half-eaten sweet roll, crumbs spilling over the plate onto the table. "What is she saying about me?"

"Don't get your knickers in a knot. She asked me to run a Men's Shed. I said no."

"Oh." Steve settled down and reached for the bun again.

Jack stroked his jaw, noting his father's flat expression and mindless chewing. "But I'm considering it."

SIENNA BACKHANDED the perspiration from her forehead as she jogged along the cliff-top road overlooking the bay. The sun was setting over the water, turning the horizon scarlet and glinting off the towers of Melbourne in the distance. Dog walkers and cyclists shared the quiet street lined on the beach side with a narrow park and the other side with large homes on leafy lots.

As a doctor she liked to practice what she preached—that the cornerstone of a healthy life was physical exercise. She wasn't fast but she was disciplined. Rain or shine she ran three miles every second day.

Footsteps thudded on the pavement behind her and she moved over to allow the runner to pass.

Instead the steps slowed. "Sienna."

"Jack!" When he fell into pace beside her she forgot everything in frank admiration of his muscular legs, ripped biceps and broad shoulders, gleaming with perspiration.

"This is a coincidence," she said to hide her confusion. "Running into each other out here."

"No coincidence. I called your house," he said. "Oliver told me where you run."

Sienna slowed her pace. "You wanted to see me? Why?"

"I've decided to give Men's Shed a trial," he said.

"You're kidding." She was so surprised she stopped running altogether.

"No, I'm serious," he said, jogging on the spot. "We'll make toys for the Trivia Night."

"That's wonderful! What made you change your mind?"

"My father. You were right—he's floundering." Jack slanted her a hard glance. "I don't want anything official, mind you. This is only temporary until Trivia Night is over. Hopefully Dad will get himself sorted out by then. I figure if he meets a few men his own age, it'll help him adjust to retirement."

"I've still got the brochures and the information I downloaded from the internet," Sienna said. "Do you want to stop by my house and pick them up after your run?"

"Sorry, no time." He started jogging backward. "I've got to clean up my workshop and get it ready for next week."

Sienna started running again. "Then I'll drop the information off next time I'm going past. How are you planning to find recruits?"

Jack ran along beside her. "I've put up notices around Summerside and spread the word among my friends."

"Sounds like you're all organized."

"Don't get the idea that I'll devote my life to this project."

"I wouldn't expect you to." Sienna ran onto the grass to avoid a woman walking her dog. "I'm just pleased you're doing it at all. You should come to the Trivia Night. It'll be fun and you'll get to see the toys you make raffled off."

"I might. Are you going?"

"Of course." She flicked her gaze sideways. His eyes were fixed on the road ahead, giving nothing away. Why was her pulse racing as if she was sprinting instead of jogging? "I'm on a team with one of my patients, Penelope, who's a teacher. I think she's filled all the other seats at our table."

"I'll sit with Sharon and Glenn." He grinned. "We'll whup your ass."

"You want to make a bet on that?" Her chin came up, and before she knew what she was doing, she surged forward, overtaking him in a burst of speed.

Seconds later he floated effortlessly past her, tweaking her braid. As his long legs carried him ahead she laughed.

Then her laughter faded. She had put childish things behind her when she'd become a doctor. When she'd taken full responsibility for her son. She needed to set a good example for Oliver…for herself.

By flirting with Jack, an unemployed charmer, she was misleading him. She wouldn't let it happen again.

FOUR MEN STOOD in a semicircle in the center of Jack's workshop, waiting expectantly for him to tell them what to do. Why had he ever agreed to do this? Right now all he wanted to do was blow off the Men's Shed and go for a bike ride.

His father, at least, was a known quantity. The others were a mixed bag. Ralph was eighty if he was a day, thin and wiry in dark blue overalls. Above the collar of his brown shirt his leathery neck disappeared into a shock of thick white hair. Bob, in sleeveless T-shirt and baggy shorts, sported a straggly dark ponytail, tattoos and an earring. He looked to be around forty and was on disability after injuring his back working as a laborer. Paul was in his fifties and, with his well-groomed gray hair, polo shirt and neat slacks, would have looked more at home on the golf course or in the boardroom. He'd been let go from his management position six months ago as a result of the economic downturn. He stood a little apart.

"Okay, guys, listen up," Jack said, more gruffly than he'd intended. He was out of practice at organizing other people. "Our project is to make toys to raffle off for the high school's new sports center. Steve knows how to make rocking horses. Does anyone else have any skills or ideas of what they could do?"

Ralph raised a shaky, gnarled hand. "I can make wooden toys. Cars, boats, trucks. I got my tools out in my truck."

"Excellent," Jack said, nodding. "Steve's brought over his lathe and I have a circular saw, so we should have woodworking covered. Bob, what's your specialty?"

Bob shrugged beefy shoulders colorfully decorated with dragons and pouncing eagles. “Dunno.”

“Do you have any hobbies?”

“Making beer.”

Over the chuckles of the other men, Jack said, “I'm not sure the PTO will let us raffle off alcohol, even to help the kids.”

Bob smoothed the soul patch beneath his bottom lip with a calloused thumb. “I learned how to make fighter kites in prison.”

“Nothing dangerous,” Jack said.

“No worries,” Bob said cheerfully. “I'll leave the metal knives and ground glass off the kite string.”

“O-kay, you can give that a go.” Jack turned to Paul. “What about you—any hobbies?”

“Polo—” He broke off as Bob sniggered. “Do you have a problem?”

“Polo? Pah-don me.” Bob put on an exaggerated English accent. “I didn't know we had royalty in the shed.”

“Cool it,” Jack said sharply and threw Bob a warning glance. “Do you know anything about bikes?” he asked Paul.

“I cycle around the bay from Brighton to Mount Eliza every Sunday morning.” The ex-executive's face brightened as he spoke.

“You're one of those wankers in Italian Lycra who ride in a pack and clog up the highway on your ten-thousand-dollar bikes,” Bob muttered.

“We're not all *wankers,* as you so crudely put it. Some of us are serious riders.” Paul turned to Jack. “Why do you ask about bikes?”

In the background Bob mincingly mimed "serious riders" to Ralph, who frowned back at him. Paul noticed. A muscle in his jaw ticked and he reached into his pocket. Jack heard a metallic clink and then he saw that the guy had two small steel balls in his palm, rolling them.

Ignoring Bob, Jack explained, "A couple of used kids' bikes have been donated, but they need refurbishing. Do you think you can do that?"

"Yes," Paul said. Clink, clink.

"Let's get started," Jack said before Bob could make any more comments. "Steve and Ralph, take the long section of the workbench. Bob, we'll clear a space at the far end, next to my electronics. Paul, why not spread out the bicycle parts on the floor over by the ultralight? I'll lend you a pair of overalls. I'll get them and be back in a minute. You boys play nice while I'm gone."

Jack crunched down the driveway and up the path to his house, Bogie at his heels. "Thank God I only agreed to do this temporarily," he muttered to the golden retriever. "We'll make a few toys, raise some money and then I'll resume normal programming. Sound good? It does to me."

Bogie nudged his hand with a cool moist nose. Jack took that as a sign he agreed and stroked the soft golden fur. Dogs were pretty darn smart.

"Do you always talk to your dog?" a woman asked, laughing.

"Sienna?" He looked over his shoulder.

There was no one there.

This was weird. She'd invaded his peace with her plans and her projects, spurring him into action. Now he was hearing her voice when she wasn't there. He'd hate to think what a shrink would make of that.

He hadn't been able to help flirting with her the other day while out running. She looked good in her T-shirt and jogging pants. Approachable. Sexy.

But he couldn't fall for a woman who regarded work as some kind of religion, a woman who would never be happy with him for who he was.

Walking faster, as if he could escape his thoughts, he let himself into the house and went through the kitchen, along the hall and into his bedroom, Bogie dogging his footsteps.

Jack slid open the closet door and rummaged through the back of the shelves among the piles of folded sweatshirts and blue jeans until he found a pair of old overalls. As he pulled them out, he knocked over a shoe box hidden among the clothes. Postcards spilled out.

His heart twisted. He thought he'd gotten rid of those. The postcards were painful reminders of the weekends he and Leanne would fly the Cessna to wherever fancy took them. As long as it had a landing strip. She would collect a card from every town they visited. She didn't write on them or mail them to anyone; she just bought them as a souvenir.

Warrnambool, Wagga Wagga… He flicked through the colorful cards. Merimbula. His hand stilled and he felt sick all of a sudden. They'd arrived at the seaside town on the New South Wales coast on a Friday afternoon. By Sunday morning when they'd departed, a low pressure system had rolled over the Great Dividing Range, bringing heavy rain.

He shut his eyes as he remembered the sound of her

voice, the things they'd talked about that day. The hopes and dreams they'd shared. All gone now. All his fault. Like his broken GPS, these postcards anchored him to the past, to his grief and guilt.

Jack shoved the postcards back into the box, grabbed the overalls and hurried back to the shed, forcing Bogie into a trot.

The scent of warm cinnamon and caramelized sugar hit him as he walked in. The men had abandoned their tools and were clustered in the kitchen area. Ralph's wife, Jean, orange haired and plump in flowered capri pants, was cutting a freshly baked coffee cake.

"Ralph asked me to make something for morning tea," Jean told Jack as she handed around big slices. She was as round as Ralph was spare and clearly pleased to have a group of appreciative men to bake for.

Steve's gaze met Jack's as he lifted a piece of cake to his mouth. His dad hesitated. Jack raised his eyebrows at his father's sheepish expression. His dad needed to lose weight, sure, but since when had he needed Jack's approval to eat?

Jack dropped the overalls on the bench and walked over to get some cake. Within a few minutes Steve was reaching for his second piece. "Go easy, Dad," he said with good humor. "Save some for the rest of us."

"Oh, don't listen to him." Jean thrust the plate under Steve's nose. "You go right ahead."

"Don't mind if I do." Steve helped himself.

A pair of boys in gray-and-green school uniforms with schoolbags on their backs appeared in the open double doorway. The curly blond head belonged to

Oliver. With him was a shorter boy with shiny brown hair that fell across his eyes.

"Hey, Oliver," Jack said. "Don't you have school?"

"We got out early because of a teacher's conference. Mum said you were starting the Men's Shed. We came to help you make toys."

"Does Sienna know you're here?"

"We stopped at the clinic on the way. It's cool." Oliver came to a halt in front of Jack. "This is Jason."

The Men's Shed was available to males of all ages, although Jack hadn't anticipated teenage boys coming along. But why not? "You boys want cake?"

Oliver's eyes lit. Jason smiled, revealing a mouth full of stainless steel braces. "Yes please," they said in unison.

Jean happily fussed over them as if she was their own grandmother.

The men had finished eating and gone back to work. Jack approached Steve, who was measuring a length of pine with a metal ruler and a carpenter's pencil. Smedley had slithered under the bench to snooze, his muzzle resting on his front paws. "How would you like to teach Dr. Maxwell's son and his friend to make rocking horses?"

Steve nodded. "Send them over."

Jack found Oliver and Jason washing their plates under Jean's supervision. "You boys go see Steve, the older man with the glasses. He's my father. He'll sort you out." The boys hurried off and Jack turned to Jean. "Thanks for bringing the cake. It was delicious."

Jean's round face was wreathed in smiles as she picked

up a tea towel to start drying. "I'll bring scones and jam tomorrow. And I make a nice pound cake, too."

"Excuse me?" Oliver was at his side.

Jack turned. "Yes?"

"I'd rather help you if that's okay. I brought some old computer disks to make robots." Oliver's soft-featured, pimply face was transformed by interest and hope.

Jack rubbed the back of his head. "I guess I could fast-track the school project I'm developing. How would you like to help me build a prototype dogbot?"

"Cool!" Oliver grinned, eyes shining. "What's a dogbot?"

The boy's eager curiosity reminded Jack of himself at that age. Something tripped over in his gut. It must be tough on Olly not to have his dad around. If Leanne hadn't died, Jack might have had a son who would look at him the way Oliver was looking at him now.

He clapped an arm around Oliver's shoulder. "That is what we're going to find out."

CHAPTER SIX

"DIABETES IS ONE of the leading causes of kidney disease—more than excessive drinking or smoking," Sienna informed the guys at the Men's Shed later that week.

She'd asked Jack if she could give a talk on men's health issues as a community service and he'd suggested she come at their morning coffee break. Standing beside her posters propped on an easel, she concluded, "I have a patient who contracted type 2 diabetes at the age of thirty-three. Without treatment, his kidneys slowly deteriorated. Now, at fifty-five years old, he has to spend fifteen hours a week on a dialysis machine just to stay alive. He can't travel or do any of the things he'd planned to do in retirement. One in four people with diabetes develops long-term kidney damage."

She glanced around the room, her gaze resting briefly on Steve. "Don't be one of the statistics."

Over the smattering of applause, she added, "Are there any questions?"

Paul, Ralph, Steve and Bob were seated on the couch and chairs. They'd listened in polite silence. Now they shook their heads—*no questions.* All through her talk Sienna had been conscious of Jack leaning against the fridge, arms crossed over his chest, watching her.

She unhooked her flip chart and started to dismantle

the stand. She hoped the men—especially Steve—had taken in the message, but it was hard to tell. "Help yourself to the fruit and veggie platter. I'll stay around for a few minutes in case you want to ask me anything."

Paul reached for a handful of carrot sticks and dipped one into the chickpea dip Jack had made for the occasion. The other men, including Steve, gravitated toward the chocolate chip cookies Jean had dropped off earlier.

Sienna left the chart stand and offered the veggie platter to Steve. "Can I have a word?"

Steve threw a hungry glance at the chocolate chip cookies, then sighed and took a few cucumber sticks and a slice of melon. "Sure."

Sienna set the platter on the table and followed him away from the others.

"A cookie wasn't going to kill me." Steve eyed the cucumbers in his hand with distaste. "Were you aiming your talk at me?"

"Not just you. Men's health is an important issue. I give the same talk to other groups in the community. But I'm glad of the chance to speak to you privately." Sienna glanced around to make sure no one was within hearing distance, then continued. "I received the lab results from your blood sugar tests. Your blood sugar is three times the acceptable level."

Behind his steel-framed glasses, fear flickered in Steve's eyes. "There must be some mistake."

"There's always a possibility these results are an anomaly," she said. "That's why standard procedure is to confirm with a follow-up test. Same thing again, on a different day."

Steve groaned. "Not more fasting."

"I'm afraid so." From her purse she produced a pamphlet and gave it to him. "Read that. Discuss it with your wife and family."

Reluctantly he accepted it, then immediately rolled it into a cylinder. "And if the next test gives the same result?"

"It will indicate you have type 2 diabetes. It's not the end of the world," she added quickly as his expression turned dark. "Diet and exercise are critical to managing the condition. Medication can improve the efficiency of your own insulin—"

"Yeah, yeah."

"You will go for the follow-up test, won't you?" Sienna pressed. "As I've just told the group, if diabetes goes untreated there can be serious complications."

"I'll get the blood test," Steve said, but without enthusiasm. "Does Jack know about the first one?"

"Not unless you mentioned it to him. Have you told your wife?"

"Nah. She's gone walkabout," he muttered. "A bloody meditation retreat."

Searching his troubled face, she said gently, "Steve, why are you keeping this from your family?"

"I explained already," he said, frowning. "I don't want people fussing over me."

Or stopping him from eating sweets, was Sienna's guess. "Make sure you take care of yourself. Are you walking?"

"Smedley gets me out every day." He bent and scratched behind the dog's ears. "Come on, pup. You need to go outside before we get back to work."

Sienna returned to the lounge area to finish packing up her display. As she was stuffing rolled posters into a cardboard tube she saw Steve detour into the kitchen, drop the cucumber sticks into the rubbish bin and tuck a couple of cookies into his pocket. Her heart sank as he left the shed. Then she shrugged. She wasn't the food police.

The other men had drifted back to work. Jack was last to go, grabbing a carrot stick and a cookie. "You hit the health message pretty hard," he said. "I think the guys are a bit shell-shocked. Food is also about enjoyment. Maybe the next time you give that talk, you might think about finding a way to make healthy food fun."

"I'm speaking to adults, not children." Sienna slid a sheaf of extra pamphlets into her briefcase. Jack looked good in his polo shirt and snug jeans but she kept her mind on business. "Does Ralph's wife bring cakes and cookies every day?"

"Pretty much. The guys really look forward to it."

Sienna hesitated. She couldn't betray doctor-patient confidentiality, but she had a moral duty to convey her concern. "Your dad would be wise to cut back on sweets. He's overweight, especially around the middle."

"He likes them." Jack's chin came up. "Doesn't everyone?"

Sienna noticed Steve, back from taking Smedley outside, watching them from across the room and decided not to pursue the matter. It was up to him to take responsibility for his health.

"All things in moderation. So, you got the shed up and running," she commented to Jack. "Are you enjoying it?"

He scowled in feigned exasperation. "Ralph puts his tools down all over the place and then forgets where. Bob needles Paul continuously. My dad's wood shavings are getting into my electronics."

In other words, he loved it. And she found the aura of purposeful energy that surrounded him *very* attractive.

"Remember, it's temporary," he warned. "Don't get any ideas."

"No ideas whatsoever." Sienna lifted her palms, careful not to say *I told you so.* "Do you mind if I take a look at what the guys are doing before I go?"

"Go ahead. I'd better go see what Oliver's up to."

Sienna left her posters, easel and briefcase in the sitting area and walked across to the workbench where Bob was making kites.

"Very impressive," Sienna said, watching Bob's stumpy fingers notch together the diamond-shaped fiberglass frame he'd constructed. Finished kites hung from the pegboard behind the bench. The colorful sails were made of ripstop nylon and appliquéd with butterflies and birds.

"My wife makes the sails at home," Bob said. "She's got a commercial sewing machine and a friend who sells her the fabric wholesale."

"You two could go into business," Sienna said.

"Nah, you couldn't make a living out of it."

As Sienna moved away, her gaze sought out Jack and Oliver. Their heads were bent together as Jack showed Olly how to attach wires to the dogbot. Olly was nodding, the way he did when he listened hard.

Jack glanced up, saw Sienna watching them. She looked away, annoyed at herself for getting caught staring.

Amid a liberal sprinkling of sawdust was a pile of rough wood blocks and a couple of wooden toy cars and boats. The layer of wood shavings carpeting the concrete floor rustled as she approached.

"Those aren't finished," Ralph said as she picked up a toy car. "I've got to give them a coat of paint."

"The wheels even turn," Sienna said, spinning a front tire. "I love the headlights and outlines of the doors."

At the end of the workbench Jack had his head down, working steadily. If he was aware of her coming closer, he wasn't letting on.

She moved on to where Steve was fitting the rockers onto a wooden horse while Jason sanded the body of another beast. A finished palomino with a painted golden body and white mane and tail stood to one side.

"Hey, Steve, Jason," Sienna said. "What a pretty horse."

Steve hiked his pants up his bulging belly and proudly touched the palomino's head to set the rockers in motion. "Jason got us real horsehair from his cousin's stables. 'Course, I know he's just hanging around the stable to chat up the girls who come to ride. Isn't that right, Jase?"

The boy flushed bright red and ducked his head, his hand flashing as he scrubbed faster with his sandpaper.

Sienna laughed softly. This time when her gaze rose she found Jack watching her. She recalled how he'd tweaked her braid. Her cheeks turned warm. Deliberately she moved away from the bench even though Olly had talked of nothing but dogbots all week. Instead she veered across the room to see what Paul was doing with the bikes.

Two used children's bikes were leaning against the wall. A third was upside down on top of a canvas tarp with the front wheel lying on the floor. Paul was hunkered down beside it, nuts, bolts and small tools organized tidily along the perimeter of the tarp.

She ran her fingers through the white plastic streamers on the handles of a pink-and-purple girl's bike. "I had a bicycle just like this when I was five years old."

Paul rose and stretched out his lower back. "You should have seen the rusted mess that was when it came in. I had to take it completely apart and spray paint every piece separately."

"You guys have accomplished so much already," she marveled. "I can't wait to see what you come up with by Trivia Night."

Paul shrugged. "We've got three weeks to find out."

Three weeks until she had to see Jack again socially.

She hovered at the edge of Paul's workspace. From the back, Jack's broad back was bent slightly as he worked, his triceps flexing below the short sleeves of his polo shirt. He stood with one hip cocked, the denim pulled snugly over his butt. Olly glanced up at him every minute or so to ask a question or get confirmation that he was assembling his robot correctly. Jack was so different from Anthony, who could perform delicate heart surgery but wouldn't know how to change a washer on a tap.

Paul stepped around her to get something and cast a

curious glance her way. Realizing she was still standing there, she took a breath and set out across the room. Her son saw her coming and made space for her between him and his new hero.

"Look at this," Oliver said, proudly placing his dogbot upright.

The toy was six inches high with a square flat body of transparent yellow plastic. It had four plastic legs attached to wheels, a black whipcord tail, a head with a steel bolt for a muzzle and pricked ears made of swiveling steel washers.

Oliver picked up a remote control and switched it on. The dogbot's head turned. Sienna smiled as Olly supplied the bark. He pressed a toggle switch and the dogbot rolled forward. "We're trying to find a way to make the tail wag."

"Your son put that together," Jack said. "He's got real talent."

"It's great, Olly." Sienna was surprised but not necessarily thrilled. She was always proud of Oliver, but lately this…talent…was distracting him from his studies.

Her ambivalence must have shown. "Something wrong?" Jack asked.

"Olly's been spending every afternoon here."

"Jack needs my help," Oliver piped up.

Sienna looked at Jack.

"That's right." Jack gazed down at Oliver and smiled.

A surge of possessiveness rushed through her. Oliver was besotted with his new friend. Jack had altogether too much influence on her son.

Get a grip. They were only making toys. It wasn't as if he had any real influence on Oliver.

She nodded at the black metal box shrouded in plastic pushed to the back of the workbench on the other side of Jack. "What's that?"

"That? Oh, nothing." There was a shimmer of tension in his voice. He leaned over to sort through a container of screws and bolts, blocking her view.

She nodded and backed off. Oliver wasn't as experienced at picking up clues or else his curiosity overrode politeness. He peered around Jack to get a closer look. "It looks like some kind of electronic instrument."

"It's just a thing I built for small aircraft," he said dismissively. "It doesn't work."

"What kind of a thing?" Oliver persisted.

"Don't bother him with so many questions," Sienna said. Although she had to admit she was curious, too. If it was nothing, why was he taking such pains to hide it?

"He doesn't mind, do you, Jack?" Oliver said.

"It's a global positioning system." He was clearly making an effort, not entirely successful, not to be irritated with the boy.

"A GPS? Cool!" Oliver put down his dogbot to scurry over.

"It's broken," Jack repeated. "Nothing to look at."

Oliver lifted a corner of the plastic. The casing was dented so badly that the components inside must have been damaged, too. The screen on the front was cracked and the control panel stripped clean away.

"It's broken, all right." Oliver touched a piece of the

screen that was sticking out and accidentally chipped it off.

"Don't do that," Jack said sharply.

Oliver dropped his hand, startled. "Sorry."

"When you say you built it, do you mean you invented it?" Sienna asked.

"I took an existing global positioning system and adapted it to cope with the requirements of small aircraft in Australia," he explained, his words hurried and impatient. "So, yes, you could say I invented it."

What he was saying sank in.

"You invented a GPS for aircraft." Her voice was flat. Gesturing to the dogbots, she demanded, "Why are you making *toys* when you're capable of creating sophisticated equipment?"

"The physical damage isn't the only problem. It's got programming bugs." He jerked the plastic cover back over the GPS. "I don't know why I haven't thrown it out."

"Couldn't you could work out the bugs?" Oliver asked.

"Not interested." Jack went back to the workbench and started wiring a battery to the underside of the yellow plastic dogbot body. A muscle ticked in his jaw as he focused intently on his task.

All of a sudden Sienna recalled how Jack had lost his wife. She put a hand on Oliver's shoulder, warning him not to ask any more questions. She glanced at the shrouded plastic and her skin prickled. Had this GPS been in the plane crash that killed her?

"I'd better go," she said awkwardly.

Jack put down the dogbot. "I'll carry your stand for you."

"I can manage..." she began, but he was already striding back to the kitchen area.

"Did I do something wrong, Mum?" Oliver asked.

"Don't worry about it. Just lay off the GPS, okay? And be home in time for dinner. I'll see you later." She ruffled his hair and let out a sigh. Then she headed across to the coffee area where Jack was gathering up her things.

Jack grabbed her briefcase, tucked her easel stand under his arm and without a word carried them out to her car. Sienna followed. She got into the driver's seat and rolled down the window. "Sorry about that back there. Oliver doesn't know..."

Jack propped his hands on the roof and leaned in. "Just what is it that you think you know?"

Sienna licked her lips, which were suddenly dry. "Your wife died in a plane crash. You were the pilot."

His features twisted. He straightened, slapped the roof. "See you around."

So it was true, Sienna thought. Jack was still hung up on his late wife.

"YOU'LL NEED A WARM HAT, gloves, ski jacket and pants—"

"I don't need ski pants," Olly said. "I'll wear jeans."

"Do you know how cold denim gets when it's wet?" Sienna stopped in the middle of the mall and peered through the throng of shoppers. "Where is that outdoors shop? I thought it was right next to Target."

"Sienna!" a woman's voice called from behind them.

Sienna gazed blankly out at a sea of unfamiliar faces. Then she spotted Lexie's blond curly head bobbing through the crowd. "Hey, Lexie."

Lexie waved at Sienna with a paint-stained hand. Over her other arm was a bag bearing the logo of an artists' supply shop. "I'm so glad I ran into you. I asked Jack for your phone number but he didn't have it. Do you remember I wanted to paint your portrait for the Archibald Prize? I was serious." She pressed her hands together. "Please, will you do it? It won't take more than a few sittings if I take photos, too. We could get started this weekend. Today, if it suits you."

"Oh, but I..." Sienna began, flustered. "Oliver, this is Lexie, Jack's sister. Lexie, this is Oliver, my son. He's going to New Zealand on a skiing trip in a few weeks. We're getting him outfitted this afternoon. Tonight I'm going out."

"You never told me that," Oliver said. "Is it a date?"

Hearing the heightened interest in his voice, she stared at him. Since when was he interested in her social life? "I'm going to dinner and a movie with Natalie, one of the other doctors at the clinic."

"Could you sit for me tomorrow?" Lexie asked hopefully.

"Well," Sienna began, racking her brains for an excuse. Sitting for her portrait seemed so vain. "I usually spend Sundays with Oliver."

"I'm working on a school project with Jason," Olly said.

In that case she had nothing to do tomorrow except wrestle with the weeds in her backyard. It wasn't about her, she decided; it was about Lexie's painting. "Okay, I can sit."

"Wonderful!" Lexie bounced on the toes of her ballet flats. Then she rummaged in her leather shoulder bag and found a scrap of paper and a pen. "Here's my address. Come around two o'clock. That's when the light hits my studio." She handed Sienna the paper. "Thank you! Thank you!"

"That's all right." Sienna smiled at Lexie's infectious enthusiasm. Getting to know her would be fun.

Lexie hurried off, and Sienna and Oliver resumed threading their way through the mall. In a few moments they came to the outdoor shop.

They searched the racks of ski jackets for something they could agree on. Oliver wanted a flashy, trendy jacket; Sienna insisted on one that would keep him warm and dry.

"How about this one?" She held up a dark brown coat.

"Ew, no."

Sienna stifled a sigh and kept flicking through the hangers. "You know you have to finish all your homework and assignments before you go, don't you?"

Oliver slipped on a bright green jacket with purple stripes on the upper arms. "This one's cool."

"And there's that math test." Sienna eyed the jacket critically as she fingered the thinly quilted down. "You'd freeze in this thing."

"I have to finish the dogbots. Jack wants to make twenty for the Trivia Night."

"The dogbots are *his* responsibility. Your job is to do your homework."

Jack this, Jack that. His name was all Sienna heard out of Oliver these days. She was trying to *forget* the man. "Why were you so interested in what I'm doing tonight?" she asked with studied casualness.

"I thought you and Jack might go out," he said with the ingenuousness of youth. "He's cool."

Sienna hoped he wasn't discussing her with her son. She held up a navy jacket. "How about this?"

"I want this one," he insisted, holding up the fluorescent-green coat. "Dad sent me the money. It's not like you're even paying for it."

"I'm still your mother and I'm sure your dad would want me to make sure you've got good-quality clothing, not junk that will fall apart or won't keep you warm."

"I'd roast in the one you chose," Oliver pointed out. "I don't get as cold as you do."

It *was* a medical fact that young people had higher metabolisms. But Sienna wasn't wearing her white coat today. "Just try it on, okay? Put on the pants, too. You want to be sure they're long enough."

"Oh, all right." Oliver took the hanger and trudged off to the fitting rooms.

She browsed through the shop, picking up a pair of ski gloves she thought he might like, then wandered back. A man in a jacket and pants just like the ones Olly had gone to try on was checking himself in the mirror outside the fitting room. Sienna was just thinking how good the outfit looked when he turned around.

The man was her son.

Her hand went to her heart. "Olly, you scared me!"

"Huh?"

"I..." She recovered and managed a smile. "I didn't

expect you to look so grown up. I thought you were a man."

He frowned importantly into the mirror. "I *am* a man." His voice cracked as he said it, though. He gave her a sheepish grin and she had to laugh.

"Go take those off and we'll pay for them," Sienna said.

Oliver's smile faded. "What about the green outfit?"

"This jacket makes you look older," she said craftily.

"They make me look *old.* Dad said to get what I wanted."

Sienna threw her hands up. "Freeze to death. See if I care."

"Cool." Oliver grabbed the other ski jacket and pants and went back to the change room.

Sienna paced outside. Oh, no, she didn't care. She would only lie awake at night wondering if he'd fallen and broken his neck. Or if he had a sniffle. Why had she ever agreed to let him go? He was too young to travel overseas on his own. Sure, his father would be there. But what if Oliver got lost on the mountain? Anthony never paid close attention to their son's whereabouts.

"Stop frowning, Mum," Oliver said, coming up to her. "You worry too much."

"Aren't you going to try those on?" Sienna asked, seeing his arms full of ski jacket and pants.

"I already did. They fit fine."

She watched him pay, conscious he was venturing further out of her orbit with this trip than ever before. Part of her was pleased he was so mature for his age.

Part of her wanted to grab him by his shirttails and hold him back.

"I got these for you," she said when he was finished paying, and presented him with a shopping bag.

Oliver dropped his own at his feet so he could examine the ski goggles, wax, a waterproof case for his wallet and mobile phone and a bright orange plastic cylinder. "What's this?" he asked, holding up the last.

"It's a whistle, in case you get caught in an avalanche."

"Mum!" Oliver laughed. "You expect the worst."

"Just make sure you wear it." She started walking off, ridiculously afraid she might start crying.

"Mum!" There was a rustle of bags and a flurry of footsteps, then Oliver's arm went around her shoulders. "Thanks," he said gruffly. "You're the best."

Blinking, she could only smile at him. *No, you are.*

And then he slipped free and his long stride carried him away, ahead of her down the mall. Teenagers didn't like to be seen walking with their mothers. She knew that. It didn't hurt, she told herself.

Well, maybe just a little.

CHAPTER SEVEN

THE DOORBELL RANG. Finally! Trivia Night had started twenty minutes ago. Jack had called yesterday to say he'd give her a ride and now he was late. Sienna hurried down the hall past Oliver's packed suitcases and stopped briefly at the mirror. Loose curls rippled over her shoulders and spilled either side of a softly clinging top that revealed a generous hint of cleavage.

Had she put too much effort into her appearance? She wished she hadn't agreed to go. He might read more into it than she intended. She reined in her anxious thoughts, took a deep breath, then let it out slowly. *Calm down.*

She opened the door. "Anthony! What are you doing here so early?"

Anthony had arranged to pick up Oliver and take him to his house for the night before their early flight to Auckland the next morning. Sienna had already said her goodbyes to Olly, expecting to be gone before Anthony arrived.

"Nice to see you, too." Her ex-husband arched one eyebrow high into his receding hairline. "May I come in?"

"Of course." She stepped back.

He walked through into the lounge room, glancing around at the modern furnishings. "I finally see your new place. Nice. Different."

"I like it." After she'd left their marital home she'd lost her taste for antiques and ornate decor.

Her ex-husband looked the same as always—tall and thin, with a slight forward lean as if he were hunting for something. His clothes, a printed T-shirt and long shorts, were more casual than usual, though. Was Anthony having a midlife crisis and grasping at his lost youth?

"Oliver's down the street at Jason's house, saying goodbye. He'll be back any minute." Steeling herself, she added, "How's Erica?"

Anthony's narrow forehead creased into two deep vertical lines. "Her blood pressure is too high. The obstetrician is considering an early inducement."

"I'm sorry to hear that." The jealousy Sienna always felt toward Erica was laced with genuine concern. "Are you sure you should be going away at this time?"

"No, I'm not sure, frankly." He ran a hand gently over his thinning hair, as if making sure it was still there. "But I promised Oliver. After backing out of our last trip I want to make it up to him."

During the summer holidays Anthony had planned to take Oliver to the Gold Coast but had to cancel at the last minute to perform an emergency heart operation. Oliver had understood, of course, but he'd been disappointed, and the fact remained that he didn't see enough of his father. Too often their designated weekends together were cut short because of Anthony's work.

"We're doing up the spare room as a nursery," Anthony told Sienna. "Decals, clouds on the ceiling, the whole shebang. Did we get rid of Olly's old cot?"

"I stored it in the attic. Just in case." Just in case a

miracle occurred and they worked out their marriage problems. How *that* would happen when they rarely talked she'd never figured out. She'd wanted another baby after Olly but had held off, not wanting to bring a child into a failing marriage.

She checked her watch. Where was Olly? Where was Jack?

"You're all dressed up. Are you going out?"

"I have a date." That wasn't true, of course, but all this talk about Anthony's new family had left her ego in need of bolstering.

"Who is he?"

"Jack Thatcher. He lives here in Summerside."

"What does he do?"

Why was that the first question everyone asked? She was probably as guilty of pigeonholing people as anyone, but it seemed unfair. Why didn't folks want to know about hobbies or friends or…or did you grow vegetables in your spare time?

"Honestly, Anthony, you sound like my father!" With a nervous laugh she glanced at her watch again.

"He's late, is he?"

"A little." Thirty minutes and counting. Was this what Jack was like? After all, he never had to be at work on time, never had a deadline to meet. He lived a carefree, unscheduled lifestyle. "Excuse me. I'll just give him a call to see what's keeping him."

"I hope he hasn't stood you up," Anthony murmured.

"He wouldn't do that." Maybe Jack wasn't used to schedules, but he wouldn't deliberately let anyone down, she felt sure of that.

She dialed his number and listened to his mobile phone ring out. Then she tried his home number. No answer. Something must have gone wrong. Maybe his truck had broken down. Maybe he'd had an accident. Maybe she should go over there and see if he needed help.

The front door opened. "Hey, Mum," Oliver called. "Dad's car is here." The teenager appeared in the doorway, his lanky body awkward and shuffling.

"Olly!" Anthony walked forward to embrace his son. "I swear you've grown two inches since I saw you last."

"Nah." Oliver ducked his head, his cheeks bright red.

"If you guys will excuse me," Sienna said. "Olly, can you lock up?"

"I'm ready to go now," he said.

"Then we'll all be off." Anthony put his arm around Olly's shoulders but his father-son camaraderie seemed forced and after a moment the boy ducked away.

Sienna hugged Oliver goodbye and issued a final volley of instructions. "Be sure to wear your hat. Don't be a daredevil. Keep that whistle on you at all times." She took a breath, blinked. "I want you home in one piece."

"I'll be fine," Olly assured her, squirming as she tried to straighten his collar. "Tell Jack I'll see him when I get back." He grabbed his bag and headed out to the street where Anthony had parked his Mercedes-Benz.

Anthony pressed a light kiss to Sienna's cheek. "You're looking good. Summerside suits you."

"It does." She smiled. "Take care of our boy."

"I will." Anthony paused. "You could give Erica a call."

Sienna wrapped her arms around herself, trying to contain the flare of anger and jealousy she felt. She'd almost been angrier with Erica over the affair than she had been with Anthony. "I'll see."

Anthony's mouth thinned but he didn't pursue it. "I'll get Olly to call you in a few days."

Sienna got her purse, a bottle of wine and a plate of cheese and crackers for Trivia Night and got into her car. She drove past the high school on the way to Jack's house just to see if he'd decided to drop the toys off before picking her up. The gym was lit and cars were pulling into the lot. But she couldn't see Jack's truck.

His shiny red ute was parked in front of the shed. The driver's door was open and the cabin light was on. Light streamed out of the building's open double doors. Inside, a radio played, the only sound in an otherwise eerily quiet scene. Sienna parked and got out of the car. As her footsteps sounded on the gravel, Bogie appeared in the shed doorway and uttered a single deep woof.

"Hey, Bogie. Where's Jack?" Sienna circled around to the back of the ute. The flatbed was loaded with bicycles lashed to one another and stacks of kites. Large cardboard boxes likely held the small wooden toys and the dogbots.

A black rocking horse lay on its side on the gravel.

Sienna righted the downed horse uneasily, her nerve endings tingling. Bogie trotted out to sniff her hand, then trotted back to the shed, pausing at the threshold to wait for her.

"Jack?" Sienna called into the building. The sound of

a groan met her ears. Bogie whined and edged toward the open area kitchen. Sienna pushed past the golden retriever. "Jack, where are you?"

"Sienna." Jack's voice was tight and hoarse, as if he was out of breath. "Over here."

His voice came from the couch, whose high back blocked her view of him. As she moved forward, she stifled a gasp. His left shoulder was slumped at a wrong angle and he was cradling his left arm with his right, holding it close to his body. Bogie whined again and licked Jack's cheek.

Sienna dropped to sit next to Jack, gently touching his arm. "You've dislocated your shoulder."

"I was…loading a rocking…horse…onto the truck." His face twisted in a spasm of pain and he paused for breath. "Bogie flushed out a possum. Damn critter shot up the back of the truck right under my nose. Startled me. My arms jerked straight up…above my head. Those horses are even heavier…than they look."

"Don't try to talk." Sienna palpated the shoulder joint. The humerus had popped out of the socket and was projected anteriorly. "I'll call an ambulance." She took her phone out of her purse.

With his good hand Jack grabbed it and tossed it onto the couch. "You…fix it for me."

"At the hospital you'll get an IV with muscle relaxants," she explained. "Then the doctor on call will relocate your joint."

"No." Jack's teeth gritted as another spasm ripped through him. "Do something now."

"I know the pain is extreme," she said in her most

soothing manner. "But once you've been treated you'll feel better very quickly."

"It's not the pain. I can handle that. It's hospitals I don't like." He paused, sweat beading his forehead. "This has happened twice before. It's an old injury. Just pop it back in place."

"I recommend you go to the hospital."

"Are you listening to me?" His glazed eyes focused sharply in a flare of anger. "I could put the shoulder back in myself if I had to. But I would have thought there'd be some perks to having a doctor on the spot."

"You'll need to go to the hospital anyway for X-rays," Sienna insisted.

"Why, so the radiologist can tell me that the anterior lip of the joint has been eroded, resulting in chronic instability? I *know* that."

"But—"

"Just push it back in, give me a couple of anti-inflammatory tablets and I'll be good to go. We don't want to be late for Trivia Night."

"You're *not* going to Trivia Night," she said, horrified.

"The hell I'm not." He glared at her.

Stubborn man. She could be here all night arguing with him. "Okay, okay." She would worry about dissuading him once his arm was back in place. "Let's get your shirt off."

Summoning a cool bedside manner, she undid the buttons. Easing first his good arm out of its sleeve, she moved behind him, pulling the shirt off his back. Years of training prevented her from gasping, but her nostrils flared as she sucked in a swift silent breath.

Three jagged scars angled across his back from his left shoulder down to his right lumbar. Lightly her fingertips traced the pale ridges marring his tanned skin. "Are these from the plane crash?"

"My arm," he reminded her, his voice tight.

"Sorry." She slipped off the other sleeve. "You need to lie on the floor," she said, and helped him into a supine position on the faded area rug.

"Have you ever done this before?" he asked.

"Many times. I did several rotations in orthopedics while I was at City Hospital." She grasped his wrist with her right hand and placed her left hand on his shoulder, her fingers obtaining firm support on the top while her thumb felt for the tip of the dislocated humerus.

"And now you're a GP in Summerside? Isn't that a bit of a comedown in the medical world?"

"Not at all. I'm chief doctor running a busy clinic instead of just another resident. Now, quiet, please. This will hurt."

"Why do you think I'm chattering like a granny at the church picnic—"

"One, two, three..." Sienna drew in a deep breath. With her right hand she carefully lifted his arm above his body, applying enough pressure to relocate the joint without damaging tissue. Supporting the head of the humerus, she gently rotated the arm and pushed the ball over the rim of the glenoid and into the socket. Sweat popped out on Jack's forehead, but he didn't so much as wince. Sienna slowly lowered his arm, gently palpating the joint to assure herself it was back in place. "How are you feeling?"

Jack struggled to a sitting position and gingerly tested the movement of his arm. "Fine."

She helped him put his shirt back on, then he batted her hand away, insisting on buttoning it himself.

"I'll get a sling out of the first-aid kit in my car," Sienna said. "We'll get you back to your house where you can rest."

When she returned a few minutes later, Jack was talking on her mobile phone. "Bob, can you get over here and help me load the rest of these toys onto the truck?" Sienna shook her head violently and he said, "On second thought, Sienna's likely to burst a blood vessel if I lift anything else tonight. I'll call Paul to give you a hand." He held the phone away from his ear, grimacing at the stream of complaints. "Yeah, well, you'll just have to work together. Stop whingeing. Steve and Ralph are too old for heavy lifting."

Sienna unwrapped the triangle of unbleached cotton. Jack had managed to do up only the two middle buttons, leaving a revealing glimpse of a tanned muscular chest and taut abdomen. She tried not to look, but now that the emergency was over she was only human.

"Sit down," she said briskly. "You're too tall for me to tie this while you're standing." She had to stop thinking of him as a man. She was a doctor, used to dealing with the most personal details of the human body with detachment and objectivity.

But this wasn't just any body—it was Jack. And the procedure felt intimate. She was all too aware of the heat coming off his skin and the nearness of his mouth. Her fingers fumbled on the last button and brushed against his belt.

"I don't need help," he said, sounding as tense as she was.

"Sit!" she barked, as exasperated with her response to him as she was with his stubbornness.

He dropped onto a stool.

Sienna reached the ends of the sling around his neck, as if she were embracing him. Where was her cool medical poise? Even with her face averted she could feel his breath on her cheek and his gaze burning her face. Her fingers fumbled as she tried to knot the cloth. Then she felt a hand slide around her waist. "What are you doing?"

"Something stupid, probably." His voice was soft and guttural.

"Jack!" she squeaked. "This is no time for non-sense."

"Shut up." He pulled her close, forehead to forehead, breath mingling. And then warm firm lips moved over hers.

Instantly lost, she began to kiss him back.

Outside a car door shut. Bogie barked once. Bob called, "Hey, dude, where are you?"

Sienna broke away, breathing hard. Jack's nostrils flared, his eyes hot and his color high.

Bob strolled into the shed. He looked from Sienna to Jack. "Whoa, what's going on here?"

"I'm tying up Jack's arm," Sienna said, fussing with the sling.

"So I see," Bob said, his expression sly and know-ing.

She ignored him and instructed Jack, "Lift your elbow. In it goes. That's right. How does your shoulder feel?"

"What shoulder?" A tiny smile tugged at Jack's mouth.

Sienna's cheeks grew warm. "I guess you'll live."

"Do you two want me to come back later?" Bob rocked on his heels, grinning and enjoying the show.

"Start loading the rest of the toys onto the truck." Sienna busied herself packing up her first-aid kit.

Luckily Paul arrived then, distracting Bob from making further jokes. Jack supervised the loading operation. Sienna got him a glass of water and anti-inflammatory tablets, which he downed in one gulp. Then with Bob behind the wheel of the truck, Jack in the passenger seat and Sienna and Paul bringing up the rear in their respective cars, they prepared to leave in a convoy.

Jack leaned out the window and looked back to give her the signal to pull out. Their eyes met and she felt a flutter in her stomach. That kiss had changed something between them. Now their attraction was out in the open. The feelings growing inside her weren't just a fantasy to be ignored or shoved aside when inconvenient. Something very real was happening here.

And it scared her to death.

JACK SURVEYED THE BRIGHTLY lit gymnasium, looking for Sharon and Glenn. His injured arm throbbed with a dull ache, but hopefully the meds would kick in soon, he thought. At his side Sienna scanned the room for her friends. He sensed she was nervous, ready to bolt. He shouldn't have kissed her. But with those full berry-red lips only a whisper away from his mouth, his brain had short-circuited. He couldn't take back a kiss. That one impulsive act could lead to complications. With another woman he might have been able to brush it off as a bit of meaningless fun, but Sienna didn't approve of him. She wouldn't have kissed him back unless her emotions were involved.

He wasn't ready for that.

Round tables seating eight crowded the polished floor. A stage had been set up at one end of the gym, where the master of ceremonies, a fortysomething man in a Hawaiian shirt, sat behind a table loaded with sound equipment. Balloons and streamers hung from the basketball hoops. Through the far door, Bob and Paul were bringing in toys to add to the pile on the tables in front of the stage.

Sienna stood on tiptoe and waved. "There's Penelope. She's a patient of mine and a teacher here."

Penelope's glossy brown hair swung as she wove through the tables to greet them. She was wearing a colorful blouse tucked into high black pants. "Finally! I was worried something had gone wrong—" She broke off, noticing Jack's sling. "What have you done to your arm?"

"It's nothing," he said tersely. "Where do we go? I'm with Sharon and Glenn Robinson."

"You and your friends are all on my table now," Penelope said. "When we found out you and Sienna were coming together we did some rearranging. Is that okay?"

Jack glanced at Sienna. She shrugged and nodded. It was only a charity night. No big deal.

"Fine. I guess," he said.

At their table sat Penelope and her husband, Barry, a

rotund man with a robust laugh; Natalie from the clinic and her partner, Deepra, a pathologist with thick iron-gray hair. The fourth couple was, of course, Sharon and Glenn.

The taped music stopped and the MC continued his patter, interspersed with trivia questions in a variety of categories. An hour and a glass of red wine later, Jack was feeling no pain. Only he and Sienna were subdued. He because of his shoulder; she—well, who knew? She glanced his way now and then, a speculative expression on her face. His thoughts and feelings were all jumbled, desire and guilt swirling in an uneasy mix. The pain in his shoulder seemed like a pointed reminder of the crash and Leanne's death, almost as if fate was telling him that what he was starting to feel for Sienna was wrong.

And yet he knew that if he got the chance, he would kiss her again.

"Now, before we have any more questions," the MC said, "we'll auction off a few of these fantastic toys made by the Summerside Men's Shed." The MC held up a dogbot and remote control. "What am I bid for this…I'm guessing it's some sort of robot."

"I'll bid ten dollars," Sienna called out.

Jack laughed in surprise. "Oliver can make one for himself. I already told him that."

"I want to surprise him. He'll be thrilled."

Either she wasn't an astute bidder or else her aim was to pay as much as possible, increasing her offer by twenty dollars at a time. When she finally got the dogbot for 250 dollars she was as pleased as if she'd won it for nothing.

After auctioning a few more items, the MC announced he was taking a short break and put on music. Sienna unwrapped her plate of cheese and crackers and set it in the middle of the table alongside the dips and vegetable sticks, tiny quiches and miniature samosas with chutney.

Jack poured Sienna more wine. "You're nuts, you know that? The parts are worth about five dollars."

"It's for a good cause." Her smile faded as she watched him adjust his sling. "Your shoulder hurts."

He hadn't been able to help that grimace, damn it. "It's fine."

"The first time you dislocated it, when you got all those scars. Was that in the plane crash?"

Music and laughter swirled around them. Glasses clinked, the aroma of savory foods filled the air. Next to him Glenn was regaling the others with an amusing anecdote about a playground incident. All of it faded away as Jack grew silent, remembering.

"Jack?" Sienna's voice seemed to come from far away.

"Yes, the plane crash." He gulped his wine, his stomach tightening like a fist. "It killed my wife. Almost killed me."

Bloody well served him right, too.

CHAPTER EIGHT

SIENNA SQUEEZED HIS HAND, quick and comforting. She left her hand in his, fingertips curling into his palm. "This isn't a good time. Forget I asked."

The gentle warmth of Sienna's fingers stirred emotions he thought he'd put away for good. He resisted them. What was the point of rehashing the past? He couldn't bring Leanne back, or…

"Hey, you two," Penelope said, interrupting the quiet moment. "I'm about to draw the raffle prizes. Get your tickets ready and listen up." Then she hurried away, up the side of the gym to the stage.

Sienna released his hand to line up he tickets on the table in front of her.

The MC took the microphone. "The first set of prizes are from the Peninsula Airfield courtesy of Jack Thatcher."

Sienna turned to him. "Oh? What are they?"

Before he could reply, the MC supplied part of the answer.

"Third prize is lunch for two at the Hangar Café," the MC announced, holding the box of tickets high.

Penelope reached inside and pulled out the winning slip of paper. "Purple, B5."

The MC repeated into the microphone. "Purple, B5."

In the audience somebody shrieked and a young

woman with short black hair leaped up, arms waving. "That's me. I won!"

She went up to the stage and received her gift certificate. The MC drew for second prize, a free skydive.

"I want that," Deepra said, perking up. "I went bungee jumping last year. Skydiving is this year's challenge."

But the winning ticket was held by an elderly man who told the MC he would give it to his grandson.

"That's okay," Natalie said, hugging her husband. "We'll play miniature golf instead."

Jack leaned across to talk to Deepra. "If you like, I'll hook you up with my buddy Jim who runs a skydiving school."

"Oh, yes, thanks." Deepra beamed.

"And now for the grand prize..." The MC hit a button on his sound equipment, creating an electronic drum roll.

Penelope fished around in the box for several seconds, drawing out the suspense. "The winning ticket for a one-hour joyride in a 1939 Tiger Moth is...Blue, D18."

A hush settled over the gymnasium as people checked their tickets. Jack alone seemed uninterested. He reached for a packet of chips, the rustle of plastic foil overloud in the quiet.

"Oh, hell," Sienna said. "I won." She tried to give it to Natalie. "Here, you take it. I don't fly unless I'm in a jumbo jet."

"I went on a joyride two years ago for my fortieth birthday. It was fantastic. Do it," Natalie urged. "You won't regret it."

"Does anyone have Blue, D18?" the MC called again.

"Go on," Sharon prodded. "Collect your prize before they draw another ticket."

Sienna rose and turned to Jack. "Will you take me up?"

"I beg your pardon?" His hands tightened around the bag, crunching the chips.

"You were a pilot, right? Will you fly the plane?" Her smile was nervous but hopeful. "The guy who owns the Tiger Moth would let you, wouldn't he? I'd feel so much better if someone I knew was at the controls."

Carefully Jack loosened his grip and set the chips on the table. "I don't fly anymore."

"What?" Sienna frowned. "Never?"

Someone, Sharon probably, again pushed her to claim her prize. Slowly Sienna moved away, looking back at him with a puzzled frown. Jack shook his head, motioned for her to go. Finally she turned and hurried to the stage.

His arm ached and inside he was ice-cold. He didn't expect her to understand. How could she know what it felt like to be responsible for the death of your spouse? After losing Leanne it was only fitting that he should also lose the thing he loved to do most—flying.

Glenn reached across for the chips, saw that the bag had popped open and poured them into a bowl. "What'd you do to these?" he asked Jack. "They're crushed to smithereens."

IT WAS AFTER MIDNIGHT when Sienna pulled into Jack's driveway. Pain was exhausting, she knew, and she could see by the glow of the security lights that his face was drawn and pale. "I'll help you inside."

"Are you going to get me into my pajamas, too?" He was tense and his attempt at humor was ironic, edgy.

"If you need help I'll contact the nursing service," she replied in kind. "Bertha is available this weekend. Six foot, she can lift you into—"

"Never mind." He backpedaled with a dry chuckle. After a moment's hesitation he added, "Come in for coffee?"

"It's much too late to be ingesting caffeine."

"Herbal tea?"

She swiveled in her seat. "You have herbal tea?"

"I have everything."

A woman could want. The thought popped into her head before she knew it was coming. "Um, okay, just a quick one."

He ushered her inside and into the lounge room and switched on an etched-glass table lamp that gave off a soft glow. "Have a seat. I'll just be a moment."

Sienna sank onto the dark red couch, then immediately bounced up to fluff her hair in the mirror over the gas fireplace and wipe away a fleck of mascara. Satisfied, she glanced around at the comfortable collection of mismatched furniture that still somehow went together. The room was clean but just untidy enough to look lived in.

She touched a framed aerial photo of mountains and frowned. Jack had gone very quiet after she'd asked him about the accident that killed his wife. Bev had said he was still in love with Leanne, and his reluctance to talk about the crash seemed to confirm that.

"That was taken near Jindabyne in the Snowy Mountains." Jack walked into the room slowly, concentrating on a pair of clinking steaming cups in his good hand.

"Here, let me get those." She took the bone china mugs and set them on the coffee table, sliding coasters beneath them. "Are you the photographer?"

"No, Leanne. I was flying the plane." He took a bottle of painkillers out of his pocket, swallowed two tablets dry and followed them with a slug of hot tea.

Sienna studied the photos. Leanne was good. Seeing the places she'd been, the images she'd taken, somehow made her feel more real. Was that why Jack kept so many on display?

"I enjoy photography myself," Sienna said. "When I find the time."

"How often is that?"

"Not very," she confessed. "Except when I'm on holiday."

"And your last holiday was…?"

"Zurich, five years ago." She thought again. "Wait a minute—I lie. We spent a week in Sydney two years ago."

"You and Oliver?"

"Anthony, Oliver and I." The trip had been a disaster from the start. She'd been making a last desperate attempt to save her marriage, but it had been clear from the beginning that Anthony hadn't wanted to be there.

Silence fell. Sienna scanned the walls for more pictures. "Do you have a photo of Leanne?"

"Why do you want to see it?"

"I just do."

Jack rose and got an album out of the bookshelf

flanking the fireplace, flipping through the pages as he walked back to the couch. "There she is."

Leanne was standing beside a two-seater plane, her outstretched hand resting on the wing. Her blond hair was cut in a shiny cap and she was wearing cargo pants and a leather bomber jacket.

"She looks adventurous."

"She was an outdoor education teacher. We met at a rock-climbing weekend she was running." Jack's voice was even, perhaps too even. He might have been talking about his next-door neighbor.

"I don't rock-climb," Sienna said, feeling inadequate.

Jack got to his feet. "More tea?"

Her cup was still nearly full, but she no longer felt like drinking it. Dead or not, Leanne was such a tangible presence she might have been sitting on the couch between Sienna and Jack. "I'd better go. It's late and I'm tired."

Without protest he walked her to the door and onto the porch. There was an awkward moment when she tried to think of something to say.

Then he spoke. "Who would have thought you were such a sports buff?"

"Or that you're a history nut." The moon had grown fatter since the last time they'd stood there together, and it rode higher in the sky, reminding her that time was always passing. "Are you still in love with her?"

Beside her, he gazed out at the sky, glowing with the moon and stars. After a long silence he said, "I'll always love her but no, not in the sense you mean."

Her heart stirred. The moment was both thrilling and

scary. It opened the door a crack. But only a crack. Why did she feel as if the memory of Leanne was holding him back?

"That night you came here for dinner I told you life was short," he said. "I live for pleasure."

She remembered. Now that she knew him better she realized he could have meant a lot of things by that seemingly flippant remark. He must have gone through many months of painful physiotherapy to recover from the accident. No wonder he put such emphasis on staying physically fit now. "Pleasure to you is about family and friends."

"That's right," he said quietly.

She turned to him and his gaze tangled with hers. She lifted her face, he bent his head. His mouth touched hers, firm and warm and sensual. She felt his hands on her waist, drawing her close. "Your shoulder," she protested.

"Stop being a doctor for a minute," he murmured against her lips.

As he deepened the kiss, she rose on tiptoe and slid her arms around his neck. Heat spiraled through her. With her hands she measured the breadth of his shoulders and tested the hardness of his muscles.

His arm is in a sling. And she was crushing it.

She started to pull away.

He held her close, both hands on her waist. With a tremor in his voice, he said, "Stay."

She was tempted. Oh, she was tempted. But she couldn't forget that they were as different as the moon and the sun.

"You're injured," she said by way of an excuse. "We shouldn't be doing this."

"I can't feel a thing." His mouth twisted in a wry smile. "Or rather, I can. But my shoulder is fine."

Sienna tried to pull away. They were torturing themselves. "If you have any trouble with that arm, make sure you call me."

Sobering, he kept hold of her hands. "What I was actually starting to say about life being short was don't be afraid—take that joyride in the Tiger Moth."

She tilted her head at his note of urgency. "Maybe I will. If you'll come out to the airfield with me."

His fingers tightened on hers, stretching the moment until she could hear the tension humming. "Y-es," he said finally, releasing her. "All right."

She walked back to her car, apprehension and anticipation warring inside her. She had the feeling they'd both just jumped in over their heads.

SIENNA WOKE THE NEXT morning feeling pleasantly, vaguely excited. Lazily she searched her sleepy mind for the reason. Oh, yes. Jack had kissed her. She snuggled deeper under the covers.

Then she recalled the joyride and it ruined all her lovely dreamy musings.

The front door opened.

Sienna started, coming fully awake. Someone was in the house. The sound of footsteps in the hall made her sit up in bed. Then she heard Oliver's voice. But what was he doing here? She listened. Anthony was here, too. He and Oliver were arguing.

She jumped out of bed, dragged on her dressing gown and hurried out. "Olly, did you forget something?"

"The trip is off. Because of *her*." Fighting back angry tears, he pushed past Sienna to go to his bedroom.

She turned to Anthony. "What's going on?"

"Erica was admitted to the hospital early this morning." Anthony had dark circles under his eyes and his clothes were creased, as if he'd spent the night in them. "Her blood pressure is 150 over 95 and there's protein in her urine."

"Preeclampsia." Sienna pressed a hand over her mouth.

He nodded, distractedly running a hand through his thinning hair. "Last night at dinner she came down with epigastric pain. We went into the hospital right away. I can't leave her."

"Of course not. Is she going to be all right?" Anthony shrugged, his mouth tightly down-turned. It was a foolish question. As a doctor she knew Erica's condition was critical. "What about the baby?"

Anthony swallowed. "They're going to induce labor."

"But Erica's only..." Sienna tried to calculate.

"Twenty-eight weeks along." Anthony's already pale skin turned white around his pinched nostrils. "I need to get back to the hospital." He glanced past her to Oliver's bedroom and the haggard lines of his face hardened. "He hasn't been very understanding. In fact, he's been a selfish little—"

"He's disappointed," Sienna said, automatically rising to Olly's defense. "It's natural."

"He's acting as if Erica got sick on purpose to spoil his trip."

"I'll speak to him." Sienna touched Anthony's arm. "Give my best to Erica."

"Thanks. I'll keep you posted."

She saw him out and then knocked on Oliver's door. "Olly, we need to talk."

"What is it?"

She opened the door. Oliver was pulling on a fresh T-shirt. "How could you be mean about Erica when she's so ill? How do you think that makes your father feel?"

"Pretty funny timing, don't you think?" His head popped through the neck hole, his thick hair sticking out every which way. "She just *happens* to get sick the day Dad and I are supposed to go away."

"Don't you think your father can tell the difference between faking and real illness?" Sienna came farther into the room, picking up Oliver's discarded shirt. "Not that Erica would fake something like this. Preeclampsia is serious. She could die. The baby could die. I can't believe you're acting like this. I'm sorry about your trip, but compared to what Erica's going through it's nothing."

"She *hates* me."

"Of course she doesn't hate you," Sienna began, then the misery of Olly's expression registered. "Did she say something? Was she mean to you?"

"Not to me," he said. "I overheard her complaining to Dad about him going off skiing. She said she and the baby are his family now." Oliver's voice broke but it was a tearful wobble, not a symptom of puberty. "Like I'm not his son anymore."

"Oh, Oliver." Sienna put her arms around him but he turned aside, refusing to be comforted. "I don't blame you for being angry. That's a horrible thing for her to say." And wouldn't she give Anthony an earful as soon as Erica and the baby were out of danger! "But when you're pregnant you feel vulnerable. She must have already been feeling sick when she said that. Don't ever think your father doesn't want you."

"If *she* doesn't want me what's the difference? He does everything she says. Every little thing." Oliver's face was pale, making the pimples on his forehead and chin stand out red and furious. "In the car all he talked about was the baby. He didn't ask me about school or my friends or what I've been doing."

"He's excited about the birth, just as he was when you were born. He wants you to bond with your stepbrother or sister," Sienna explained. Anthony had good intentions where Oliver was concerned, she knew that, but his execution was clumsy.

"The baby's not even born. How can I bond with it?" Oliver brushed past her and headed for the front door.

"Hey, guess what?" Sienna said, following him down the hall. "I won a joyride in a Tiger Moth airplane at the Trivia Night. Do you want to take the flight instead of me?"

"No, thanks," he grunted. Grabbing his jacket from a hook, he pushed his feet into his running shoes without undoing the laces. "I'm going to Jason's."

Sienna caught him by the arm. "Listen, Olly, I know you're upset, but now that you're not going to New

Zealand you could take that math qualifying exam tomorrow with the rest of the students."

"I'm not going to school tomorrow." Oliver shook her off and reached for the doorknob. "If I was skiing I wouldn't even be here."

"That's not acceptable and you know it," she said, furious. But short of engaging in a scuffling match she couldn't prevent him from leaving.

"Whatever." Oliver jammed his hands in his pockets. Head down, he spun off the steps in one long stride, shoulders hunched up around his ears.

She hurried after him in her dressing gown as far as the sidewalk. "Come back here."

He kept on walking. Sienna clenched her hands into fists hidden by her blue satin sleeves. The man who lived on the corner was walking his bulldog. Across the road, a car had pulled up and an elderly woman emerged. They both glanced her way, curious.

Gritting her teeth, she waved at Oliver, pretending nothing was wrong. "See you later."

Gathering the skirts of her dressing gown, Sienna ran back up the steps, seething. He'd never openly defied her before. And he wasn't going to get away with it.

She got out her address book and rang Jason's mother. "Hi, Lisa. It's Sienna Maxwell. I'm sorry to call so early. Oliver's on his way over. Could you send him home, please?"

CHAPTER NINE

SIENNA SLID THE PAN of her homemade lasagna into the oven. It was Oliver's favorite—and one of the few things she could cook.

Hands on hips, she glanced at the clock and frowned. It was nearly five and he wasn't home from school. The Men's Shed was finished, so he couldn't be there. His advanced math exam had been today and he knew she'd be anxious to hear how he'd done.

Yesterday, when he'd gotten home from Jason's, he'd apologized for being rude, then he'd sulked in his room for the rest of the day. This morning he'd mumbled and groaned and stomped out the door to school, his shirt untucked and hanging below his pullover in defiance of school rules.

Sienna didn't condone his behavior with regard to Erica, but she understood. He wasn't just disappointed at not going skiing; he felt rejected by his father and jealous of the new baby. Between lasagna and the dogbot she hoped to make him feel better.

The front door opened and shut. Sienna listened for the sound of Oliver kicking off his shoes. As they hit the wall she winced, thinking of the smudge marks. Today she wouldn't chastise him.

"Hi, Olly," she called, expecting him to come directly into the kitchen to forage for food. "I made lasagna."

He muttered something, but the sound was distant as if he was down the hall, halfway to his bedroom. Sienna shrugged and finished rinsing the dirty pots. When he hadn't emerged after fifteen minutes, she went looking for him.

He lay with his face to the wall, turning the pages of a magazine, music blaring from his CD player. "Will you turn that down, please?" she said loudly.

Oliver rolled over, stabbed at the volume control, then rolled away from her again.

Sienna took two deep breaths, telling herself not to get angry. "How did you go on the math exam?"

He just shrugged.

"Why were you late?"

"I was with Jason."

Getting information out of this kid was like pulling teeth. Sienna thought wistfully of the days when he talked nonstop. "At his house?"

"No." Oliver flipped the page of his magazine. Cars, of course. In another year he could get his learner's license. That thought scared the life out of her.

"Olly, would you please look at me when I'm talking to you?"

"What do you want?" he asked without turning to her.

"Dinner will be ready in half an hour."

"I'm not hungry."

Her head jerked, she was so surprised. "Since when are you not hungry?"

He made no reply.

"Oliver, what's going on?" She stepped over the books

and dirty clothes on the floor to touch his shoulder. “Are you sick? Let me feel your forehead.”

At the tug of her hand he reluctantly flopped over onto his back and glared up at her. The reason stood out immediately. On the right side of his upper lip was a piercing. Oliver’s downy young flesh had been perforated by a stainless steel spike.

“Oh, Oliver.” She pressed her fingers to her own lips, the wind knocked out of her. It looked so ugly, so painful. “How could you do that to yourself?”

He sat up and swung his legs off the bed. His chin rose. “It’s cool. Jason got one in his eyebrow.”

“If Jason walked off a cliff, would you follow him?”

“It was *my* idea.”

“But…you have to be sixteen years old to get a piercing without parental permission.”

Oliver’s defiance drained away. He scuffed the toe of one sock foot against a crumpled piece of paper on the floor. “Jason’s brother made us fake ID.”

“He what!” Sienna could feel her blood pressure rise. “Hand it over, right now.” Oliver dug a plastic-coated card out of his pocket and gave it to her. She looked at the card. “Eighteen! I suppose you thought you’d go into a pub and buy beer.”

“No!” Oliver jumped to his feet. “I don’t know why he made us eighteen instead of sixteen. Jeez, Mum, what do you think I am?”

“I don’t know anymore, Olly. You never talk to me—”

“’Cuz you’re always yelling—”

“I am not—”

"You're doing it now!"

Sienna closed her eyes and drew a deep breath. Letting it out, she opened her eyes again and said more calmly, "I'm a parent. It's my job to yell when my kid does something this foolish. There's no way you look eighteen. I'm going to have a word with the owner of this piercing place. Where is it?"

"In the city."

"You went all the way to Melbourne?" Her mouth opened. He must have taken the train. But he couldn't have gone to the city and back in the short time after school. "You skipped classes to do this."

"It's no big deal."

"It's a very big deal. Your grades are slipping. You can't afford to miss class."

"If I'd been on the skiing trip I wouldn't have been in school at all."

"Don't keep harping on the ski trip. That's completely beside the point." She sucked in a breath. "The exam!"

"Missed it."

"You what? That's it. You're grounded for a month."

"A month!" he wailed as if she'd given him a life sentence.

"Don't think you're getting out of the exam," she said, stabbing a finger in his direction. "I'll call your teacher and arrange for you to take a makeup test. Now, get washed up. Dinner will be in twenty minutes. And don't you dare tell me you're not hungry."

"I am. But I'm not supposed to chew for three hours and I can't eat hot food for twenty-four hours."

"I made *lasagna*." She didn't have to add that she'd

made it for his sake. He would know that. But instead of looking remorseful his face flushed with resentment.

She strode out, shutting the door behind her. Hard. Angry tears pricked at her eyes and she dashed them away. He was changing, and not for the better. Skipping school, insolence, the piercing. She hated to say it, but things had gone from bad to worse with Oliver ever since he'd started hanging around the Shed and spending time with Jack. Thank goodness that was over.

JACK TIDIED THE REMNANTS of the toy-making enterprise in his workshop. Now that the Men's Shed and Trivia Night were over, it was good to have his life back again. But it sure was quiet.

Hampered by the sling, he took it off and tossed it onto the back of the faded couch. His shoulder still hurt, but it was nothing he couldn't handle. Bogie flopped on the area rug in the sitting area, muzzle on his front paws, his liquid brown eyes following Jack's every move.

Small things had been left behind—a few blocks of wood from Ralph's toy boats, scraps of colorful fabric and string from Bob's kites, empty paint pots Steve had used. In Paul's work area, a can of WD40.

Whatever was still usable Jack put aside, and the rubbish he piled in cardboard boxes to go out with the trash. It was *nice* not to have to listen to Bob needling Paul. Or Steve and Ralph jawing about how life was so much better back in the '60s and '70s. He would be able to concentrate. Still, as he passed the radio he flipped on a talk show.

The commentator's words flowed in the background as Jack's thoughts turned to Trivia Night. He hadn't spoken about Leanne in a long time. But he had to admit it hadn't hurt as much as he'd expected. Sienna was compassionate but she didn't gush with pity, and it helped that she was an outsider who hadn't known and loved Leanne.

Sienna seemed less and less like an outsider all the time, though.

He'd like to do something to repay her for fixing his shoulder. Taking an interest in Oliver might count—except that was no hardship. The boy was everything Jack would have wanted in a son.

After he had all the large pieces of rubbish gathered up he brushed down the workbench of sawdust, string and metal filings.

When he came to the shrouded GPS some impulse he didn't want to analyze made him set down his dustpan and brush and peel the plastic covering off the metal casing. If he *was* going to fix it, the first thing he'd need to do after replacing the damaged casing and components would be to reprogram the satellite signal receiver—

Footsteps crunched on the gravel driveway. Jack slipped the plastic back over the GPS. He *wasn't* going to fix it. So what was the point of even looking at it?

Oliver hovered on the threshold, hands in his pockets, shoulders hunched. "Hey, Jack."

"Olly!" Jack said. "I thought you'd gone skiing."

"Dad had to cancel. My stepmother is sick." He explained the situation in a few bitter words.

"I'm sorry to hear that." Jack glanced past Oliver for his buddy. "Where's Jason today?"

"He's got an orthodontist appointment." Oliver

glanced around the empty workshop. "Where is everybody?"

"The Men's Shed is finished now that Trivia Night is over. Didn't you know that?"

"Yeah. I just thought..." He trailed off with a shrug. "I thought they'd stick around anyway."

Jack massaged his bad shoulder. Bob had hinted that he'd like to make more kites. Ralph and Paul had seemed disappointed, too. Jack had put them all off. The Shed was temporary, damn it. "What's that in your lip?"

Oliver touched the steel spike sticking out of his red swollen skin and grimaced. "It's a piercing. I think it might be infected."

"You should get Sienna to look at it... What does she think of you getting a piercing?"

Oliver dropped his gaze. He scuffed the toe of his black leather school shoe. "She doesn't like it much."

Jack just bet she didn't. "What made you do it?"

Oliver shrugged. "Dunno." His gaze roamed over the end of the workbench they'd shared. "Did all the dogbots sell?"

"Ye-es," Jack replied warily. From the wistful expression in Olly's eyes he surmised that Sienna hadn't given her son the dogbot she'd paid a small fortune for. It could have something to do with that bit of steel sticking out of Oliver's lip. Or not. If she was saving it for a special occasion he'd better not spoil the surprise.

Jack's arm was aching after his exertions, so he nodded at the broom in the corner. "How about giving me a hand cleaning up?"

"Sure." Oliver set to work. "What happened to your shoulder?"

Jack put the sling back on and explained how the injury occurred and how Sienna had fixed it. "It was pretty handy having a doctor in the house."

Oliver swept in silence. Dust flew in a small cloud around the head of the broom.

"Bummer about the ski trip," Jack ventured.

"I didn't really want to go anyway. I was just doing it 'cuz my dad wanted to."

"I see." That wasn't the impression Oliver had given in the days leading up to the trip. "I'm sorry to hear about your stepmom. I hope it's nothing serious."

"It's pretty bad," Oliver admitted grudgingly. "She's pregnant and had to go into the hospital early." He swept Paul's area even though Paul had left it spotless. "Did that black-and-red BMX sell? That was cool."

"It was raffled off. Don't you have a bike?"

"I left it at my dad's place so we could go riding when I visit him." His eyebrows pulled together in a scowl. "We won't be doing that *now,* though."

O-kay. Oliver was in trouble with his mother and mad at his dad. Jack walked over to the fridge and brought out a couple of cold cans. "Want a soft drink?"

"Sure. Thanks." He popped the top and drank. "I'm thinking of getting my tongue pierced next," he said, full of bravado.

"Lots of blood vessels in the tongue," Jack observed mildly. "A high concentration of nerve endings, too. That's got to be a painful place to get pierced."

Suddenly Oliver looked a little less certain, if not downright ill. "We could start up the Men's Shed again, couldn't we?" he asked, changing the subject. He waved his soda can at the workbench and tools. "I'll bet there are lots of projects we could do."

Jack's heart gave a funny lurch at the "we" and all it implied. "I've got a lot of stuff to do in the next few months." He had nothing coming up. Why was he making excuses?

"Oh. Right." Oliver put his can in the bin and went back to sweeping.

Jack watched him a moment. "You can still hang out here whenever I'm around."

Oliver lifted his head. "And make electronic stuff?"

"Sure. I've got an old voltmeter you can have. I'll show you how to make a simple circuit board and you can play around with that at home."

"Cool. Now?"

"You finish sweeping and I'll get the things." Jack went to his shelves and took down a box of spare circuit boards and odds and ends.

Oliver dumped the dust and put the broom away. Over the next couple of hours Jack showed him how to solder wire, and how to set up and test an electromagnetic circuit, light a tiny bulb and a few other basics. "What grade are you in again?"

"Nine." Oliver pressed a switch, delighting in seeing the lightbulb glow.

"Do you like school?"

"I *hate* it," Oliver said with a passion that startled Jack. "Math, English, biology, they all suck. I can't wait until I'm old enough to quit."

"Quitting isn't an option at your age. But you might

prefer a different type of school when you're a little older," Jack said. "Have you thought about technical college?"

"I don't know anything about it," he said, touching the voltmeter leads on either side of the lightbulb to test the strength of the current.

"You can learn a lot of practical things. I left school when I was sixteen and did an apprenticeship in airplane mechanics. Later I took electronics courses."

Oliver put down the leads and stared at Jack. "You mean you didn't finish grade twelve?"

"I've found that for me, the best way to learn is by doing. Never be afraid to get your hands dirty."

The boy's face lit up. "I *like* getting my hands dirty."

"That's the spirit," Jack said. "The trades need smart young guys like you. You'd have to be willing to work hard, though."

"Oh, I would," Oliver assured him. "How do I start?"

"In a couple of years you'll be able to sign up for introductory courses in whatever field you're interested in. Then once you get an apprenticeship you take more courses at the same time as you're working and earning money."

"Cool." Oliver's eyes gleamed. "I want that."

There was a lot of Sienna in Oliver, Jack thought, glimpsing the determined man Olly would one day become. If only she could see him right this moment, full of enthusiasm and a sense of direction. And here she thought her son had no ambition.

His mobile phone, lying on the kitchen counter, rang. "Excuse me," he said to Oliver and went to answer it. "Hello?"

"Is Oliver there?" Sienna asked.

The sound of her voice sent an unexpected charge through him, as if he'd touched a damp finger to the battery Oliver's circuit was hooked up to. "Yes, he's here."

"Didn't he tell you he was grounded?"

Jack looked around at Oliver. *"Grounded?"* The boy froze, then his mouth screwed up and his gaze dropped. "I'll send him home right away."

Jack hung up and shook his head. "Why didn't you tell me you were grounded?"

"I just wanted to hang out. Sorry." Oliver put down the battery and copper wire. Shoulders slumped, he picked up his backpack.

"Aren't you forgetting something?" Jack asked.

"Thank you for showing me all that stuff," Oliver replied politely.

The boy tugged at Jack's heartstrings and at the same time he had to bite his cheek not to smile. How could one kid elicit so many different emotions? "You're welcome. But I meant your voltmeter and circuit board."

Olly grinned sheepishly, his one lip quite swollen. "Oh, yeah. Thanks. Thanks a lot." He carefully stowed it all in his backpack. "See you..." He trailed off. "Sometime."

"OW! IT STINGS." Oliver, sitting on the closed toilet seat, tried to jerk his head away.

"Hold still, Olly. You should have come to me with

this sooner." Crouched before him, Sienna dabbed the antiseptic-soaked cotton ball on the swollen skin around his piercing. "I talked to your teacher. You're doing the makeup math test next Tuesday."

"I wouldn't need advanced mathematics if I went to a technical college."

"Technical college?" Sienna laughed. "Wherever did you get such an idea?"

Oliver started to speak, then closed his mouth.

Sienna made a couple more dabs, then sat back. "If you take the post out and let the hole grow over you won't have this problem again."

"I'll take better care of it," he said, reaching past her to the counter for the antiseptic mouth rinse.

"Well, mind you do. You don't want the infection to get so bad you have to go on antibiotics. You could have scarring and who knows what hideous disfigurement."

"You're just trying to scare me."

"Is it working?" She gazed intently into his face, pretending to look for signs of fear.

"No." His lips twitched. For a moment they almost shared a smile. "Can I watch TV?"

She dropped the cotton ball into the bin. "No, you're going to study for your math test. But I'll make you a deal. Take the piercing out and I'll unground you."

Oliver relapsed into a sullen frown. "No."

"Suit yourself." Sienna turned on the tap and washed her hands. The sooner he got accepted into advanced math, the better. Then they could start looking at his course selection for next year. Technical college, indeed.

"OH, MY GOD," Sienna muttered as she watched the Tiger Moth do a loop-the-loop against the cloudless blue sky. She and Jack stood at the end of the runway, waiting for the pilot to come down. Butterflies as big as the 1930s biplane were having a dogfight inside her stomach. "It looks even smaller in real life than it did on the website."

"It's beautiful," Jack said reverently.

Sienna slid him a sidelong glance. His head was tilted back and he'd rocked onto his heels as he tracked the flight path of the tiny plane. He had a look of heightened awareness and keen concentration. Whatever else he'd lost the day of the crash, it wasn't his love of flying.

The Tiger Moth straightened out and started to descend.

"Are you sure you won't fly the plane?" Sienna asked. Jack didn't seem to hear her. "Hello. Earth to Jack?"

"Huh?" He turned to her, blinking. "Sorry, did you say something?"

"Are you sure you won't pilot the Tiger Moth?"

He shoved his hands into his pockets. "Nah, not interested."

"Really? I saw your face just now."

"I don't know what you're talking about."

"Maybe you don't want to fly the plane, but you could go up. Here, you take the ticket." She tucked it into the front pocket of his shirt.

He put it straight back into her purse. "Are you chicken, Dr. Maxwell?"

"Me, chicken? Just because the Tiger Moth looks like those toy balsa-wood planes Olly used to put together and fly with the help of a wound-up elastic band?"

"Cluuuuck, cluck, cluck, cluck." She had to swat him on the arm to make him stop.

"Oh, dear, was that your sore arm?" she asked, knowing full well it wasn't.

"No, it's okay."

"Damn. Turn around and I'll have another go."

He twisted, grabbing her by the waist and pulling her close so she couldn't strike. He kissed her, hard and fast, surprising her into a breathless smile.

"You're going up and you're going to love it. See you in an hour." He started to walk away swiftly.

The Tiger Moth had landed and was slowly rolling across the tarmac toward them.

"Where are you going?" she called, taking a few steps after him. "Aren't you going to stick around?"

"There's a metalwork shop over in Hastings. I'm going to pick up some supplies while I'm down this way."

"For your ultralight?" she asked, hoping he'd been inspired.

"For the stovepipe of my wood-burning heater." He gestured to the hangar. "Don't worry about the loop-the-loop. Mac's just showing off. He won't do that unless you want him to." With a brisk salute he turned on his heel and headed to his truck.

"What the hell?" she wondered softly, watching him drive off. She would understand if the crash had made him afraid of flying, but she would swear that wasn't it. He *longed* to be up there.

"Good morning," a tall bald man with a Scottish burr called out. "Are you the lucky raffle winner?"

She turned to see Mac, in tan pants and a black

leather bomber jacket, striding toward her, two brown leather helmets tucked beneath his arm. He was about fifty years old but with the rangy physique of a much younger man.

She swallowed. "Lucky. That would be me."

As she walked behind Mac to the Tiger Moth the butterflies in her stomach began to nosedive. She barely heard what he was saying, catching just enough to know he was cracking some wildly inappropriate joke about falling out of the sky.

Mac glanced over his shoulder and grinned. "I'm not making you nervous, am I?"

"No." She smiled gamely. If only Jack was beside her, holding her hand, this might not be so hard. As it was, her heart was racing and her palms were sweating. Commercial flights on jets were fine; she could pretend she was in a large safe building. But a small plane with only a thin shell between her and the earth hundreds of feet below?

She put on the leather helmet Mac gave her and then posed stiffly, one hand on the battered metal fuselage, while he snapped a souvenir photo of her. All the while she could feel pressure building in her chest.

She climbed a wooden step onto the bottom wing, ducking to avoid bumping her head on the top wing. She started to get into the rear cockpit, but Mac motioned her to the front. Worse and worse. The door was a rectangular flap of metal that folded down instead of sideways. Swinging her leg over, she slid into the padded leather seat, so low she could barely see over the side.

She wiped a hand across her clammy forehead. *No one ever died of an anxiety attack. I can be anxious and still deal with this situation.* But her stomach was roiling, her breath was short, leaving her dizzy and light-headed. What if this wasn't panic? What if she was actually having a heart attack? *I am in control of myself and my feelings. My feelings aren't controlling me.*

Yeah, right.

Then Mac lowered heavy straps over her shoulders, weighing her down, holding her firmly in place. Her heart began to race. In spite of knowing all the right things to do, she *couldn't* deal with it. She *wasn't* in control.

"Let me out!" she said, frantically struggling to undo the buckles. "I have to get out."

CHAPTER TEN

JACK FOUND HER in the coffee shop, her hands curled around a mug, her shoulders hunched up to her ears as she stared out the window at a Cessna Skyhawk taxiing down the runway for takeoff. He signaled to the waitress behind the counter for a cup of coffee, then dropped into the chair opposite Sienna. "How did it go?"

She saw him and smiled brightly. "Lovely! Great, really great! Fantastic!"

He eyed her. "You didn't go up, did you?"

Her shoulders slumped as she dropped the act. "No."

"Are you that afraid of flying?"

"I had a panic attack." She turned her mug around, her short-nailed fingers flexing, agitated. "No offense to Mac—I'm sure he's extremely competent. Panic attacks aren't very rational."

"Has this happened to you before?"

She glanced up, clearly troubled. "I used to get them when I was going through my divorce."

Jack nodded to the waitress as she set his coffee on the table and topped up Sienna's cup. "I suppose that's another situation where you weren't in control?"

"You make me sound like a control freak."

"I'm just putting two and two together."

Sienna shrugged and reached for a packet of sweetener, shaking the crystals down.

Jack stirred cream into his coffee, studying her. "It's over. So why are you still tense?"

"I'm *not* tense," she said, ripping the packet so hard the sugar substitute spilled over the scarred red Formica. "I just don't like failing."

"Or what you perceive as failing," Jack suggested. "What made your marriage break down?"

"My ex cheated with another woman."

"Then he's scum."

"He's not scum," she said reluctantly. "I tried to do everything right. I still couldn't make my marriage work. The question is, *why* did he cheat?"

"Because he's scum."

She rose abruptly. "I've had enough coffee. This is my third cup and my hands are starting to shake. I'll wait for you outside."

Jack watched her go, shoulders squared, head high. She was so hard on herself. But anyone who would cheat on her *had* to be scum.

He paid for the coffee he hadn't drunk, then pushed through the glass door to join Sienna at the edge of the tarmac. A Piper Cherokee was taking off, its engine revs increasing as it trundled down the runway, increasingly faster until takeoff. Now the plane was climbing, the wings rocking slightly, buffeted by the wind. Jack could almost feel the lift and vibration through his body.

"What's your story, Jack?" Sienna asked. "Why don't you fly? You're clearly longing to get up there."

Her question brought him to earth with a thud. "Look

at the time," he said, glancing at his watch. "We'd better get going."

Without waiting for a response he started striding down the gravel path to the parking lot, his running shoes shooting small stones into the weedy grass.

Sienna hurried to catch up, her springy hair bouncing. "How did that crash happen? Was it caused by the GPS?"

"I don't want to talk about it."

"I would respect that if I wasn't so certain you *need* to talk about it. Do you feel guilty or something?"

He glanced at her. "Are you my therapist now?"

"Do you need one?"

Hell. "Okay, yes, it was the GPS, the instrument I designed and built. It was faulty. When I needed it most, it stopped working."

"How..." she began.

"It's complicated," he snapped. "It broke and I didn't notice because it reverted to dead reckoning mode."

"What—"

"What does that mean?" he cut in. "It means it looks like it's working when it's not. Leanne and I were talking. I was distracted."

Jack, honey, we're going to have a baby.

The memory hit him hard—he could almost hear her voice inside his head. He stopped, needing a moment just to breathe. His anger and impatience, which had been holding him together, drained away.

"Jack, are you okay?" Sienna asked.

"When it came time to land, I believed I was at the airstrip." Jack faltered, his gut tightening as he recalled with stark clarity the moment before impact. When he realized, too late, what had happened. "I lowered the landing gear. And flew straight into an escarpment."

"Oh, Jack." Sienna touched his arm—she might even have stroked it. He couldn't feel a thing.

"When I saw that cliff face coming at us I hauled on the controls with everything I had, trying to gain elevation." His arms tensed, fists clenched, as if he was even now trying to work the controls. "Then a strong gust of wind caught the plane, twisting it so that the passenger side hit first."

"Leanne—"

"Was killed instantly." Even to his own ears, his voice sounded robotic. "I sustained multiple fractures and internal injuries that kept me in the hospital for six months."

"Oh, my God. That's so awful." She squeezed his arm. "It's a miracle you survived. I'm so sorry about Leanne."

He rubbed a hand over his face. It took an extraordinary effort not to fall apart.

"Was it just you two in the plane?" Sienna asked. "Were there any other casualties?"

Jack couldn't breathe. The way the controls had crushed his ribs. Leanne had lain broken in the mangled wreckage of the copilot's seat.

"No," he lied. "It was just the two of us."

THUNK. SIENNA'S RIGHT front tire ran over something on the road. She was on the way home from the clinic, tired and hot. Her mood worsened as she pulled to the curb, the car bumping along. She got out to look and her heart sank. Great. A flat tire.

She reached for her mobile to call the automobile association. The phone wasn't in her purse. She must have left it on her desk at work. Could anything else go wrong today?

She should try to change the tire herself. But she was ashamed to admit she'd never done that and she wasn't about to start learning while wearing her good silk blouse. She would walk. It was a nice day and her house was only a mile away.

A mile was nothing—except that she was wearing new shoes. They'd felt comfortable when she left the house this morning, but by the time she got home her heels and the sides of her small toes were blistered.

Inside the front door she pried the tight shoes off her swollen feet and limped down the hall. Olly's books, jacket and schoolbag were scattered from the front door to the kitchen. There, the breakfast dishes he was supposed to tidy up still sat on the counter.

"Olly!" Sienna knocked on his bedroom door before opening it. "You've left a huge mess. I hope you're studying."

He was cross-legged on the carpet in front of a two-foot square of plywood strung with wires. He had the metal probes of some sort of meter hooked up to either side of a lightbulb.

Her hand tightened on the door frame. "*What* are you doing?"

"I'm testing the amount of current going through the bulb." Olly touched the probes to the bare wire on either side of the bulb. "See the needle move? That's the voltage."

"Where did you get that thing?"

"Jack."

Sienna took in a deep breath, struggling to control her annoyance. "I know I sound like a broken record, but you need to concentrate on studying for your math test, not play with silly gadgets."

"It's a real voltmeter," Oliver said, his face flushing. "I'm practicing for when I go to technical college."

"Don't start that again. Now, crack those books. I'll tidy up and start dinner." She started to leave, then a thought struck that stopped her in her tracks. "Wait a minute. Did *Jack* tell you about technical college?"

Wariness stole over Oliver's face. He began coiling the wire on the voltmeter probes. "Maybe."

"Tell me, Olly," Sienna demanded. "What nonsense has he been filling your head with?"

"It's not nonsense," Oliver said. "*He* quit school at sixteen to do an apprenticeship. Why can't I?"

Jack hadn't graduated from high school?

Her fingers tightened on the door frame. "Did he tell you to quit school?"

"He didn't say that, not exactly." Oliver opened his schoolbag and started pulling his notebooks onto his desk.

"But he encouraged you to apprentice?"

"Yes," Oliver said. "But only because I *want* to."

All this time she'd been grateful for the attention Jack was paying Olly. Meanwhile he'd been undermining her efforts to keep her son on track academically. He *knew* she was worried about Olly. How dared he go behind her back and try to influence him away from a medical career?

"I'm going to call him right now," Sienna said, clenching her hands into fists. "This has got to stop."

"Mum, you can't," Oliver pleaded.

"Just watch me." Pushing up the sleeves of her silk blouse, she marched to the phone. Gripping the receiver, she stabbed at the number pad. "It's time I made it perfectly clear where your future lies."

"He's not at home," Oliver said from the doorway. "He kayaks on Tuesday afternoons."

Blowing out an exasperated breath, she slammed the phone back on the hook. "Then I'll track him down at the beach. You get on with your homework."

She shoved her feet into sneakers and stalked out to the garage, her irritation growing by the minute. Then she stopped dead at the empty space. *Damn.* She'd forgotten about the flat tire. Well, that wasn't going to stop her. Wheeling out her bicycle, she set off.

JACK'S PADDLE SLICED through the water and rose in a smooth rhythmic motion as he kayaked parallel to the shore. Drops sprayed off the blade and glistened in the afternoon sun. He wore a half wet suit, which kept his core warm but left his lower arms and legs bare. His shoulder had hurt at first, but after twenty minutes of paddling, his muscles were warm and almost pain free.

Blue sky, sunshine, sparkling water. To his left was the town's namesake, Summerside Beach, a crescent of white sand between two rocky cliffs. Brightly colored bathing boxes lined the shore to the sailing club, where the sand was littered with beached dinghies, kayaks and sailboards. To his right, the expanse of Port Phillip Bay, and in the distance, the Melbourne skyline.

He wished Sienna could experience this with him. She needed more pleasure in her life, needed to relax.

Hearing someone calling, Jack glanced over his shoulder toward the beach. A hundred meters away at the water's edge stood a small trim figure with long red hair. Speak of the devil! He was too far away to hear what she said, but he grinned. Sienna was bouncing up and down, waving her arm at him. Make that two arms. She really knew how to say g'day.

He waved back, then balanced his paddle across his kayak and cupped his hands around his mouth. "I'm coming—" He broke off, eyes widening in surprise.

Sienna was hauling a kayak from the sailing club down the beach and into the water. A man came out of the clubhouse and called, but she ignored him. When the kayak was floating she kicked off her shoes, rolled up her pant legs and waded out with the water lapping at her bare knees.

What on earth was she doing? Jack shielded his eyes to see, chuckling as she tried to climb into the rocking kayak. Each attempt succeeded in pushing the kayak farther offshore until she was waist-deep. Then heaving herself up, she flopped on her stomach across the cockpit and dangled there a moment before sliding helplessly back into the water. It was like a comedy sketch.

Jack set off, paddle flashing, to help her. Before he was halfway, Sienna somehow managed to scramble into the tippy craft. She fished the floating paddle out of the water and set off. What her technique lacked in finesse was made up for in energy. Jack had never seen anyone paddle so hard to so little purpose. With every stroke she veered first one way, then the other. The distance covered after some minutes of frantic activity amounted to practically nil. He slowed his own pace just to watch her crazy efforts, not troubling to hide his enjoyment.

As he came closer and he began to make out the shape of her features, his grin faded. That wasn't a smile she was wearing; it was a scowl. She wasn't happy to see him—she was angry. In fact, judging by the sparks shooting out of her eyes and her red cheeks, he'd say she was furious.

"What's wrong?" he said when she was close enough to hear him.

Strands of wet hair were plastered to her cheeks. Her blouse was sticking to her breasts and he could make out the lacy outline of her bra beneath the transparent fabric. It wasn't the time to be taking note of such things, but he couldn't help it. Then she saw the direction of his gaze and he could have sworn steam hissed out of her ears.

"Don't you dare ogle me!"

"Wouldn't dream of it." He lifted his gaze, only to be impaled by a lethal glare.

"What do you think you're doing?" she demanded.

"Uh..." Somehow he suspected "kayaking" wasn't the correct answer. "Why don't you tell me?"

"You told Oliver..." she began, jabbing the air with her paddle. The violent movement put her off balance and set the kayak wobbling dangerously. She tried to counterbalance and the rocking increased. Water sloshed into her cockpit, and she flailed the paddle around, her eyes wide. "What is it with these crazy boats?"

Jack reached out and grabbed the hull of her kayak to stabilize her. "Relax and the boat will steady itself."

"How can I relax? It's going to slip right out from under me!" A choppy wave from a passing motorboat rocked the kayak. Panicking, she dropped the paddle and clamped her fingers around his biceps.

"Careful!" he said. "You'll end up dunking us both. If you feel the kayak rolling over, do a somersault underwater and slide out."

"What if I get stuck?" Sienna's furious gaze flashed back to him. "This is all your fault."

"I was coming to help you!" They were literally an arm's length away. "It's not my fault you're hotheaded."

"*Everything's* your fault," she fumed.

Jack bit down on a grin. Maybe it was the unevolved male in him, but he enjoyed seeing Sienna with her chest heaving and her eyes flashing. He had the urge to haul her into his arms, kiss her senseless, then tease her until she laughed. "What, specifically, is my fault? Something about Oliver, I take it."

"You told him to do an apprenticeship!" Her kayak rocked violently. She grabbed his other arm.

"I did suggest he might enjoy that," Jack agreed, relieved it was something simple. "He's a natural with electronics. I'd be happy to mentor him."

"You are not going to mentor him. He is not going to miss out on an advanced education to be a tradesman." Sienna was gripping both of Jack's arms now and they were twisted to face each other, hanging over the water, both kayaks tilting at a dangerous angle.

"There's nothing wrong with being a—" Jack began.

"He's going to be a *doctor…*"

Jack doubted that very much, but he managed to stop himself from rolling his eyes.

"Or at least he's going to graduate university so he has *options,*" she continued. "I won't let a decision he makes as a teen affect the rest of his life."

Jack shipped his paddle and held her arms to prevent them both from falling into the water. "What sparked all this?"

"I found Oliver playing with some meters and wires you gave him. Now he's talking about quitting school and doing an apprenticeship. He said you were going to help him."

Jack looked down. The gap between the kayaks was widening. He spoke faster. "I didn't tell him to quit school. I simply encouraged him to develop his natural talents."

"He said *you* left school at sixteen." Sienna looked at him as if he'd grown two heads and they were both writhing with snakes.

"It's no big deal," he said, irked by her disapproval. Jack was starting to think this wasn't so funny. In fact, it was a mystery how he could have been so attracted to this woman. "Don't you think Oliver can decide what's right for him?"

"He's too young to decide. It's not that long ago he wanted to run away and join a circus." Glancing down, she saw how precariously they were balanced. Of course the moment she tensed up, the kayak began to slide out from under her. "Holy crap," she whispered, clinging to his arms. "What do we do now?"

"Put your arms around my neck," Jack said. "I'll pull your boat toward mine."

"Is this a trick?" she demanded. But she inched her hands up his arms, wiggling her fingers into his armpits.

"Hey," he said, squirming. "Don't tickle."

"I can't help it. I'm trying to keep my head above—" With a shrill cry, she lost her grip and pitched forward out of the kayak, falling into the salt water with a huge splash.

Jack nearly overturned but managed to right himself at the last second with deft paddlework. Sienna surfaced, gasping for air and blinking furiously, her hair streaming over her eyes. Before he could stop himself, he let out a guffaw.

"Are you laughing at me?" she fumed.

"N-n-no," he sputtered, shoulders shaking.

"I'm *drowning* here!" She looked like a wet cat, mad as hell and itching to scratch his eyes out.

She was treading water, churning the sea so hard that her shoulders were above the surface. He pushed over her floating paddle. "Just don't hit me with it."

"I can't even lift it out of the damn water." Her mouth screwed up and for a second she looked as if she would cry. Then all at once a chuckle escaped. Then another. Soon she was giggling uncontrollably. Only, she wasn't happy, Jack realized; she was hysterical.

"Give me your hand," he said. "I'll help you get back into the boat."

She reached up to clasp his outstretched hand. Her fingers tightened. Then with a sharp tug she pulled on his hand and rolled his kayak. His yelp of surprise was lost as he sank beneath the water. Years of experience kicked in and Jack slid out of the kayak in a smooth somersault. He opened his eyes underwater to see Sienna's face just below the surface, peering down at him, her cheeks full of air and her hair floating like seaweed.

When he surfaced, she popped up, too. "I wanted to see how you do that somersault."

Jack shook his wet hair back, blinked the water out of his eyes. "You're nuts. Certifiable."

"I've had the *crappiest* day! You would not believe how bad my day was. And now *this,*" she said, lifting her hands, palms up. "I'm wearing my good clothes *in* the ocean."

"Sienna, look around you," Jack said, trying to get her attention. "Look at the light, the sky, the sparkling water."

It was early evening, his favorite time of day, when the setting sun cast a warm reddish glow on the bathing boxes and the cliffs.

She took in he surroundings. Droplets sparkled on her eyelashes. Faint freckles stood out on her wet nose. Captivated, Jack drifted closer. When he kissed her, her lips were moist and tangy with salt. For a moment she started to respond.

Then Sienna pushed him away, her irises a vivid, changing green, reflecting the choppy sea. "I'm still mad at you."

CHAPTER ELEVEN

TREADING WATER, Jack tilted one end of his overturned kayak to drain it, then rolled it right side up. Placing a hand on either side, he hoisted himself up, legs tucked, and swiveled, sliding inside. He turned to Sienna. "I'll hold your kayak while you get back in."

"Not in a million years am I getting back in that boat."

"You can't swim to shore in those clothes."

"You're right." She began undoing the buttons at her waist and stripping off her pants. They tangled around her ankles and she had to duck under the water to pull them over her feet. She stuffed them inside the kayak, then undid her blouse.

Jack wolf whistled through his teeth.

She whipped off the pale blue silky fabric and flung it at his face. Then she set off swimming for the beach. "Not a bad stroke," he said. "With a little training you could be a swimmer."

"I came second in the state championships in high school."

"You didn't come first? I'm disappointed." He retrieved her clothes, attached a tow rope to the bow of her kayak and followed her. "Want a tow to shore?"

She blew a jet of salt spray at him and swam on. A few minutes later she found her footing in the shallows and rose, water sluicing off her coral-colored bra and panties. The setting sun gilded her creamy skin and set fire to the long wavy hair streaming down her back.

Botticelli's Venus, Jack thought, lost in admiration. This was how Lexie should have painted her. Maybe not in her underwear, but coming out of the sea.

Jack beached the kayaks and dragged them ashore, then took hers close to the sailing club. He'd left a towel on the beach next to his pile of clothes. Unzipping his wet suit to the waist, he let his torso air dry and gave the towel to Sienna, still trying to control his grin. "You should have seen your face when your kayak went over."

"Laugh away, dolphin boy," she said, drying herself off with brisk rough strokes. "I had no idea these things were so tippy. No idea." She sneezed and picked up her shoes. "How I'm going to ride my bike back up that hill in wet clothes, I don't know."

"I'll throw the bike in the back of my ute." He wrapped the towel around her wet shoulders and picked up his kayak. "Come with me."

He loaded his kayak and her bike onto his utility truck. As she brushed the sand off before getting in, he noticed the blisters. "What did you do to your feet?"

"I had a flat tire and had to walk home." She sneezed again.

"Hop in," he said, climbing into the driver's seat in his wet suit. After she did, he started the truck and drove off up the hill. At the top she told him to turn left. Jack entered a newer subdivision where the mansions came with tennis courts, swimming pools and a view of the bay. "I should have known you'd be in the posh end of town."

"Keep driving, James."

She directed him to the oldest part of Summerside, down a narrow road where tall cypress trees arched overhead and the 1950s summer homes of Melbournites, now quaint compared to modern dwellings, were set far back from the street. "Ah, now, *this* is what I call a nice neighborhood."

"Here we are, on the left."

He pulled into her driveway and parked in front of a single-story wooden house painted white with green trim. The wraparound veranda was crowded with pots of white and red geraniums. "Get changed and we'll go get your car."

"You don't have to do that," she protested between sneezes. "Anyway it's down the road. And you're wet, too."

"I'll be fine. Go, before you catch pneumonia." He slanted her a stern look. "Doctor's orders."

"But..." she began, then stopped. "Okay. Thanks."

She hurried into the house. While she was gone Jack stripped down to his bathing suit and put his shorts and T-shirt on. Sienna appeared a few minutes later wearing dry jeans and a pullover and carrying two cups of coffee in travel mugs. Back in the truck, she directed him to her car. Jack pulled in behind and parked.

Sienna got out and opened the trunk of her car. "I would have changed the tire myself when it happened, but..." She trailed off as she awkwardly removed the jack from where it was wedged beneath the spare tire.

"But?" he prompted, reaching down to lift the spare out of the way for her.

"I was in a hurry."

"To get to the beach and chew me out?"

"No, I wasn't mad at you at that point."

He watched her put the jack in the wrong spot beneath the wheel well and waited for her to realize it. But first she had to study the handle and figure out which end slotted where. She was too proud to ask him to change the tire for her and he wouldn't dream of insulting her by taking charge. Jack leaned against the car and sipped his coffee. The afternoon's entertainment wasn't over yet.

She crouched next to the jack and tried one end of the handle. It didn't fit. She glanced over her shoulder at him and her eyes narrowed as she saw his smirk and realized he knew she was doing it wrong. Her cheeks grew red, but she seemed even more determined to succeed.

"We need to talk about Olly," she said, turning the handle around. "He looks up to you. What else was he going to think when he heard you didn't finish school?"

Jack waited until she'd gotten the handle positioned properly before replying, "That a person can be a success despite not graduating from high school?"

Dropping to a crouch, she began to crank the jack. "Would you call yourself a success?"

Implied insults aside, he couldn't let her ruin her paint job. "Stop. The jack goes in that slot to the left of the wheel well." Nudging her aside, he let the car down the half inch she'd raised it and moved the jack to the correct position.

"Why didn't you tell me in the first place?" she huffed.

"You seemed bent on doing it yourself. You've also got to loosen the nuts on the wheel before you go any further. As I'm sure you know." He got the wrench from the trunk and gave the nuts each a twist to start loosening them—otherwise they'd be here all night. "Are you saying I'm not a success just because I didn't finish grade twelve and go on to higher education?"

"Look at you!" She began to turn the jack handle again. "It's midweek and you're kayaking as if you haven't a care in the world."

"So I have a great lifestyle. What's wrong with that? Maybe you're jealous. I don't condemn you because you can't cook."

"Who says I can't?" Her head came up, red hair springing like a ruffled bantam rooster.

He would have laughed if he'd been feeling amused. "You did. Not in so many words, but it was implied."

Sienna cranked furiously. She was kneeling on the pavement now, heedless of her clean jeans. "You *had* something with the Men's Shed. Then you quit just when it was getting really good."

"The Shed was your idea, not mine," he pointed out.

"But you liked it."

He didn't want to talk about that, or about the sudden void the Shed's closure had left in his life. "This isn't about me. It's about Oliver." He set his cup on the roof of her car. *"Isn't it?"*

"Yes, of course it's about Oliver." She floundered, realizing she'd gotten off track. "I wouldn't be doing my job as a parent if I didn't make him finish grade twelve in the academic stream."

"Academics aren't right for everyone."

"They're right for Oliver," she insisted. The wheel was off the ground now. She threw down the jack and used the wrench to finish loosening the nuts. There was grease beneath her short scrubbed nails and her hair was falling in her face.

"Why don't you let the boy's talent and his inclinations decide what his profession should be?" As she removed the nuts Jack set them in a safe place on the curb. "Do you want me to finish changing the tire?"

"No, thanks." Embracing the tire in both arms, she wrestled it off the axle. It came free suddenly and she sat down hard on the curb.

"He's got an analytical mind. And he's good with his hands," Jack said, helping her to her feet. He took the tire and rolled it over to the rear of the car.

"He's a healer at heart." Her voice was fierce with motherly love.

"But he wants to learn robotics." Jack handed her the spare.

"He's forever bringing home birds with broken wings, possums that've fallen out of their mother's pouches, salamanders that've lost a tail," she said as she dragged the good tire to the front of the car. "Well, he used to. He has more outside interests these days."

With a lot of grunting and cursing, she managed to heave it up and onto the axle. When it was done she straightened and looked Jack in the eye. "I know my son. I want what's best for him."

"I'm sure you do." Jack was frustrated because he could see her side, but she couldn't seem to understand where he was coming from. "But how good a parent are you if you don't pay attention to what Oliver wants?"

"He's too young to know."

"*I* knew at that age."

"And look at you now." She twirled the nuts back into place on the bolts. "Just because you're not fulfilling your potential is no reason to encourage Oliver to settle for less than he's capable of."

"Whoa!" Was she *trying* to make him angry? "So we're back to talking about me now?"

"I'm just calling it like I see it." She tightened the nuts with the wrench, then turned the jack handle the opposite direction to bring the car down.

"Forget about *your* ambitions for him," Jack said. "Think about what will make Oliver happy."

She straightened and planted both hands on her hips. "Happy isn't about playing at your hobbies all day. It's about living a productive life."

"I *have* a productive life." He glared at her.

Her eyes locked with his. "I was talking about *Oliver*."

Jack picked up the flat tire and stowed it in the trunk. To hell with her feminist sensibilities. The sooner he got out of here, the better. When she would have put the wrench away, too, he took it and gave the nuts another few turns to tighten them properly.

Sienna put away the jack and slammed the trunk.

"Unless you're a parent, you can't understand. You don't know what it's like to have a teenage son."

Jack flinched as though she'd slapped him. "No, I don't," he said, his voice tight. "You've got that on me."

"So do I have your word you won't try to influence him?"

He got into his truck, started the engine and lowered the window. "Since he can't visit me, and I'm not allowed to talk about our mutual interest in robotics even if I run into him on the street, I'm not likely to have much influence, am I?"

SIENNA SNEEZED AND PRESSED a tissue to her runny nose. She had a cold, and standing in Lexie's drafty studio with nothing but a blue bedsheet draped around her naked body wasn't helping. "Can I turn the heater up?"

"Don't move." Lexie, a clutch of brushes in her left hand, dabbed at the portrait with quick short strokes. "I'll get it in a minute." Belatedly she added, "Bless you."

Sienna let her gaze drift to the window again, half hoping, half afraid Jack would show up. Hoping? Had she really thought that? She didn't care if she never saw him again.

"He's not coming over today," Lexie said. "I mentioned you'd be here. He said he'd be sure to stay away."

Ouch. Lexie thought her brother was being thoughtful; she didn't know the reason behind Jack's absence. But it was Sienna who had a right to be angry, not him.

Lexie twirled a brush in the jar of turpentine then absentmindedly wiped it clean using the hem of her loose paint-smeared shirt. "I heard you two had a great time at Trivia Night."

"It was okay," Sienna conceded reluctantly. Jack had been at his most charming that evening until she'd brought up the crash. She could see how *some* women could fall for him.

"I also heard you were a hero and fixed his dislocated shoulder." Putting down her brushes, Lexie walked over to turn up the space heater on the floor next to Sienna.

"That was nothing." She waved it away and then brightened. "The other day I changed a tire." A blast of warmth curled around her ankles and she stretched her cramped toes. "Well, with a little help."

"And you two went out to the airfield together," Lexie continued. "That's the first time he's been around planes since the crash."

"Really? I didn't know that. I could see it wasn't easy for him." Which made it rather special that he'd gone for her sake.

Lexie wagged a finger. "See, I know all about you and Jack. I'm thrilled you two are dating."

"We're not dating," Sienna corrected her. "Far from it."

"But I thought—" Lexie began.

Sienna's phone made a distinctive chirp, saving her from explaining. "Excuse me, that's Oliver." Reaching into her purse at her feet, she retrieved the phone and read the text message. "Typical. He wants to know what's for dinner." She messaged back Leftovers.

"You're so lucky," Lexie said. "I'd love to have a kid."

Sienna studied Lexie's averted face with the smudge of red paint on one cheek. "You still have time. You'll meet someone."

"Maybe. I'm nearly thirty-eight and the clock's ticking."

"Hey, ladies." Renita, wearing a flowing tunic over loose-cut pants, knocked on the open door and came into the studio.

"Renita, I'm always happy to see you," Lexie said, then threw her a pointed glance. "Except when I'm painting."

"I know, I'm sorry. I just came from Jack's house." Renita ran a hand over a splattered wooden chair testing for wet paint, decided there was no risk, then sat. She turned to Sienna. "He said you two had a fight."

"What?" Lexie said to Sienna. "You never mentioned that. What happened? Is that why you're not dating anymore?"

"We were *never* dating," Sienna said. "Why does everyone think we were?"

"Because you do things together," Renita said.

"Look, he's very handsome and charming and fun to be with, but—"

"I can see how that would put a person off, don't you?" Lexie said to Renita.

Sienna threw up her hands. "Are you two that desperate to hook your brother up with someone? He doesn't seem to have trouble attracting women."

"Oh, they hover around him like wasps on plums," Renita said. "The problem is finding someone who'll challenge him, someone he won't get bored with." She beamed. "We think you have potential."

"Well, I'm sorry, but it's not going to happen."

"What did you fight about?" Lexie asked.

"I had a go at him for encouraging Oliver to do an apprenticeship when I want my son to go to med school," Sienna said. "Jack took our conversation personally. He was offended by my remarks about his lack of higher education. I know university isn't the be-all and end-all," she added, adjusting her toga. "But Jack and I have completely different goals and ambitions." As in *she* had goals and ambitions and *he* had none.

"Jack built a successful air charter business," Renita said. "What difference does it make what route he took to get there?"

"He's not in business now. He let it go. He's not even doing the Men's Shed. It was all set up and running and he just dropped it." Sienna got steamed up just thinking of the waste. "Anyway, it wasn't all one-sided. He insulted me, too."

Lexie stopped painting, brush held aloft. "What did he say?"

"Oh, well, just that I can't cook." It was true, of course, but *he* didn't know that. The more she thought about it, the more annoyed she became. He was making assumptions about her when he had no idea. *No idea.*

"You can't let him get away with that," Renita said, laughing. "Invite him to dinner. Show him what you can do."

"Ooh, yes!" Lexie chimed in. "We'll come, too."

"Lexie!" Renita said. "You can't invite yourself."

Renita and Lexie were trying to matchmake; Sienna

knew that and dismissed it. But giving dinner parties was high on the list of what Sienna hoped to achieve in Summerside. She should learn to cook. Her culinary skills were deficient and she wasn't satisfied with being less than stellar at anything she attempted. Inviting Jack, having to prove herself, would provide incentive. She wouldn't become a gourmet cook overnight, but she was willing to try. When a person tried, success often followed. It sure didn't happen by sitting on your duff.

"I'll do it," Sienna announced, her mind already working out the details. "You can both come and bring dates. I'll invite my friends Glyneth and Rex." Sienna glanced from Renita to Lexie. "Okay?"

"Okay!" Renita and Lexie agreed in unison.

"Excellent." Sienna stood up. "Lexie, would you mind if we took a rain check on this sitting? I need to get organized if I'm going to throw a dinner party. It'll take me a few days."

"Sure, no problem," Lexie said. "Good luck with Jack."

She didn't need luck, Sienna thought as she drove home. She needed a plan of attack.

JACK CHECKED HIS WATCH for the umpteenth time since he'd dragged himself out of bed at 11:00 a.m. It was only three o'clock. Too soon to call anyone to meet him at the pub for a drink. Anyway, all his friends would be working.

He'd taken Bogie for a run, stocked his pantry, tidied his house, updated his Facebook page, checked on his stocks and read the newspaper from front to back. Plenty of excitement for one day.

He prowled the house, looking for something to do. Anything.

The Men's Shed had ruined him for a life of leisure, he realized. He missed the guys. Missed having something productive to show for his day.

Damn that Sienna Maxwell.

Thinking of her made him chuckle. She wanted to be so perfect. He couldn't wait to see her come up against something she couldn't handle. Couldn't wait for her to fall flat on her face. He couldn't wait to see her admit she wasn't perfect at everything she attempted. He couldn't wait to—

He couldn't wait to see her.

Hell.

It was this house. Apart from his run, he'd been cooped up all day. He needed to get out, to do something, talk to someone.

Jack grabbed his car keys and wallet and fled. He got into his ute and started driving, not knowing where he was going. As he passed his father's house, he slowed. With Mum away he really should check on Dad more frequently. The old man wasn't himself these days. He used to be busy around the farm literally from sunup to sundown. Now he had nothing to do and no idea how to fill his day.

Jack parked in the driveway and walked up the path to the door. He knocked and went in. "Hey, Dad. It's me."

"In the living room," Steve called.

The house was dim, the curtains drawn. Jack followed the blue glow from the TV to find his father burrowed in his recliner, watching an old John Wayne movie. An empty cookie packet sat on the table next to his chair. Smedley lay across Steve's legs. Even for a small pooch, he was too big to be a lapdog and his sheepish expression showed that he knew it. Not that he was going to budge.

"What are you doing?" Jack asked. "Want to go for a walk or something?"

"Nah, I don't feel so good," Steve said. "I'll just stay here."

Jack sat on the couch and leaned forward, elbows on his knees. "I heard our toys raised over two thousand dollars for the school athletic center."

Interest flickered over Steve's face. "That right? Is there going to be another fundraiser, do you know?"

"Not that I've heard." Jack watched the cowboys tear through the canyon while a lone Apache watched from atop the cliff. "We don't need a fundraiser. We could make something in my workshop."

"What?" Steve asked.

"I don't know. Didn't our cousin in Sydney just have a baby? We could make him a rocking horse. Or was the baby a she?"

"Your mother would know." Steve fondled Smedley's ears. "It wouldn't be the same without all the guys."

Jack nodded, twisting his hands together. "So what are you doing this afternoon?"

"Sittin'." Steve shrugged. "Nothing else *to* do."

"You could go visit Ralph. "

"Maybe." A commercial came on. Steve flicked through the channels.

"Jeez, Dad. You can't just sit around all day, doing nothing!"

Steve turned his face toward him. At that angle Jack saw not his eyes but the reflection of the TV screen in his glasses. "What are *you* doing that's so all-fired important?"

Jack stared at him, at a loss for words.

JACK ADJUSTED the gooseneck lamp so that it shone directly onto the computer motherboard. Tucking his tongue between his teeth, he carefully lowered a microchip into place with a pair of jeweler's tweezers. After he'd left his father's house, Steve's words had alternated with Sienna's over and over in his brain. *What are you doing that's so important? Would you call yourself a success?*

He wasn't going to apologize for talking to Oliver. She was wrong about her son; Jack had no doubt on that score. She was wrong about him, too, and her assessment of him still stung. He wasn't going to change on *her* say-so.

He was only in his workshop because he'd glanced through an aviation engineering journal and had an idea of what might have gone wrong with his GPS program. If it didn't work, no big deal. His father, though, now there was a real problem that needed to be fixed.

The radio was on low in the background and Bogie was snoozing beneath his feet when he heard the crunch of gravel beneath tires and headlights hit him full in the face through the workshop window. Jack glanced at the clock, saw it was nearly 10:00 p.m. and wondered who would come calling at this hour on a weeknight.

The headlights went out, a car door slammed and footsteps approached. Bogie was at the door first. His warning bark gave way to a wagging tail and wriggling body as he greeted the new arrival.

Sienna.

Thanks a lot, Bogie, you traitor.

"Hey, Boogie-woogie." Sienna's voice was a low croon. "How's my boy?"

She straightened away from the dog and Jack noticed she was all dolled up. Her long burnished ringlets were held loosely back and she was wearing a clingy wrap-around dress and high-heeled sandals. An unexpected jolt of jealousy stabbed his gut. The late hour, the hair, the makeup. Had she been out with another guy? Not that he cared.

He jammed his hands into his back pockets, conscious he was wearing his oldest work pants, the pair with the hole in the knee, and a sweatshirt with frayed cuffs. "What's the occasion?"

"No occasion. I was just passing. Thought I'd stop in." Her voice was breathless and her gaze darted about, from him to the workbench to the kitchen, as if she was nervous. "Am I interrupting?"

"No, come in." Deeply ingrained manners overrode his wounded pride. "Want some coffee?"

"No herbal tea?"

"The Shed is man country. We don't drink herbal tea. It's plain black or nothing."

"I won't have anything, thanks." She twisted the strap on her shoulder bag with manicured fingers. "I came by to apologize. I said things I shouldn't have."

His shoulders stiffened, but he waited to hear what she had to say.

"You did a really good job with Men's Shed," she went on. "You're not a—"

Don't say it. He clenched his hands inside his pockets.

"—failure."

"I don't need a pep talk."

"Sorry. I just… Sorry."

Silence fell. The jazz station played an old Charles Mingus tune in the background.

"What are you working on?" She glanced along the bench, checking out what he was doing. Despite what she'd said, he knew that in her eyes he was a failure no matter that he had money, hobbies and friends. To her, success was narrowly defined as career achievement.

"Upgrading Renita's home computer," he said, banking on her not knowing the difference between a personal computer motherboard and the inner workings of the GPS. Bogie nudged at his leg and Jack reached down to pat him. "How's Olly?"

"He's fine." Mention of Oliver brought a moment's awkward silence. Then she went on in a rush, "I came by to invite you to dinner. Lexie and Renita are going to be there and my friends from Melbourne. Next Saturday. Can you make it?"

She was handing him an olive branch. The question was, did he want to take it? They'd quarreled over fundamental issues. The Men's Shed was finished and he would have no further contact with her son. Was there any point in continuing to see each other?

Curiosity alone made him ask, "Thai chicken curry?"

"It'll be a surprise, but whatever it is, it'll be great."

She lifted her chin, flicking her hair behind her shoulder. "I'm going to show you that I can cook."

Reluctantly he smiled. "This I've got to see."

"So you'll be there?"

Still he hesitated. An anxious frown knit her brow. A look like that was hard to resist.

"I'll be there."

His eyes strayed to her lips. It had been days since he'd kissed her. And the way that soft dress clung to her breasts…

"I'd better go." It was as if she'd read his thoughts. "See you Saturday." Turning, she swayed back to her car, one arm flung out to balance herself on her high heels in the gravel.

Jack scratched his head, not quite sure what to make of this new twist in their *un*relationship.

CHAPTER TWELVE

"MUM, ARE YOU COOKING AGAIN?" Sniffing the smoky air, Oliver came into the kitchen, his backpack slung over one shoulder.

Sienna put down the spent fire extinguisher and flapped a dish towel at the black clouds billowing from the top of the stove. "I need to get rid of the smell before my guests arrive."

Oliver cranked open the long narrow windows of the family room, letting in a rush of cool air that made the smoke swirl. "What *is* that thing anyway?"

Sienna fought back tears as she gazed at the blackened lump rising from the sea of foam that blanketed the stove and kitchen counter. "Chinese smoked duck."

"It's definitely smoked," Olly agreed.

"It took me all day to prepare it," Sienna moaned. "Overnight, if you count the marinating."

The recipe had seemed straightforward, if lengthy. She'd steamed the duck, smoked it in tea leaves in a wok and then deep-fried it. That was when the skin caught fire.

"Maybe if you scrape off the burned bits you'll still be able to eat it," Oliver suggested.

"There'll be nothing left! Olly, what am I going to do?"

"Make lasagna. Even you don't stuff that up."

"It's so mundane. I told Jack I would make something wonderful. I let him think I can cook."

"That was dumb." Oliver hoisted his pack. "I'm going to Jason's. *We'll* be having pizza."

"Just because I'm ungrounding you for the evening doesn't mean you're allowed to taunt me." Sienna snapped her dish towel halfheartedly at him. "Go, before I change my mind and make you stay home and wait on us. See you tomorrow."

She dumped the charred bird into the garbage bin in the garage and made sure the lid was on tightly. The smoke was clearing, so she lit some candles to get rid of the odor. But what would she do about a new meal?

She'd set the table earlier with her best china, silver and crystal. It was more formal than Jack's house, but this was the way she did things. Tonight was supposed to have been perfect.

She put the dirty pots and pans in the dishwasher and wiped down the counters. Standing in the glow of the fridge light, she ruminated on the meager contents. What fabulous meal could she whip up in less than an hour from half a dozen eggs, ketchup and leftover rice?

She could look up another recipe, buy more ingredients… There was no time. She shut the fridge door and paced the kitchen. Panic ate at her. After hyping herself so much, she couldn't crash and burn in front of Jack.

Oh! She had an idea. She could zip down to Instant Gourmet and be back with three courses before the first guest arrived. Okay, so it was cheating. So what? No one would ever know.

Half an hour later Sienna carried in shopping bags

loaded with a feast. There were fresh oysters and Ligurian olives, spatchcocked quail with fancy French lentils and something rich and creamy for dessert.

She'd just got all the food out of the Instant Gourmet containers and into her own dishes for heating and serving when the doorbell rang. Hastily she ran out to the garage and dumped the containers into the bins. Then she walked slowly to the door, breathing deeply several times and smoothing back her hair.

She opened the door. "Glyneth, Rex. It's so good to see you."

Glyneth, a tall and willowy brunette in a designer dress and heels, hugged her fiercely. "You look fabulous. I like your hair down! And I love your new place." She poked her head into the lounge room. "It's small but very cute."

Sienna turned to Rex, a short, barrel-chested man with a graying brush cut. His hand-tailored jacket and Italian shoes wouldn't have looked out of place in the finest restaurant. "The Jag didn't act up?"

He wrapped her in a bear hug. "Purred like a kitten the whole way here. Looking good, kid." Releasing her, he handed over a bottle of wine. "We left home early in case there were any more car dramas. Are we the first?"

"The others will be here soon." Sienna went to put their bottle in the fridge and removed a sparkling pinot gris, already chilled.

"Something smells delicious." Glyneth followed Sienna into the kitchen and lifted a lid on a casserole dish. "What is it?"

"Um…" Sienna racked her brain. What was the

French name for the lentils? She felt guilty about not coming clean with Glyneth, but her friend might think it was hugely funny and let everyone in on the joke. "It's Puy lentils with um, pine nuts and…currants. The grilled quail are keeping warm in the oven."

Sienna picked up wineglasses and motioned with her head for them to follow. "Rex, can you bring the olives? Let's go into the lounge room. It's less messy."

"What are you talking about?" Glyneth said, glancing around at the gleaming tiles and granite counter. "Your kitchen is immaculate. A person would never know you'd even been cooking."

"Well, I have. All day." Just not these dishes. "It's more comfortable in here." Sienna set the wine bottle down and began to arrange white porcelain bowls of crudités on her dark wood coffee table.

Glyneth picked an olive and popped it into her mouth. "So where's your hunky man?"

"What makes you think I have a man?" Sienna twisted off the cork, then remembered that the sparkling wine was supposed to go with the oysters. Luckily for her, Instant Gourmet recommended and stocked wines to accompany every course. "Just a minute, I'll get the amontillado."

"Amontillado," Glyneth repeated with a knowing grin directed at Rex. "She wouldn't go to this much trouble if she wasn't trying to impress a man."

Sienna recapped the sparkling and put it in a wine chiller, then went to an antique Chinese cabinet for the bottle of Spanish sherry. "I don't need a man to go to some effort. Cooking is my new hobby."

Glyneth took another olive and waited, one eyebrow arched skeptically.

"It is," she insisted, unable to admit the truth, even to her good friend. She wanted to be a gourmet cook and she would become a gourmet cook. Her smile started to feel strained.

"And what about the man?" Glyneth persisted.

"Jack and I are barely friends, let alone in a relationship."

"Then why did you invite him?" Glyneth asked.

Because even though she knew he was wrong for her, she wanted to see him. It was that simple and that dumb. "It's all very complicated."

"Complicated is interesting. We like complicated." Glyneth patted her husband's pudgy hand. "Don't we, Rex?"

"I prefer simple, myself," Rex said, popping a feta-stuffed pimento into his mouth.

The doorbell rang again.

"Oh, goody," Glyneth said, rubbing her hands together.

Renita arrived with Martin, a short man with sandy-colored hair who worked at the bank. Then Lexie breezed in with Peter, a musician friend with blond dreadlocks.

The next fifteen minutes were a flurry of introductions and getting-to-know-you chatter. Sienna made sure everyone had a glass of sherry and refilled the olive bowl. Nervous, she perched on the edge of her chair and tried not to gulp her drink. She'd never hosted a dinner party on her own. To make matters worse, she wasn't serving her own food. She was cheating.

The doorbell rang. Sienna hurried to open it and found Jack on the doorstep, all rumpled dark hair and sexy grin.

A wave of relief and pleasure that she wasn't prepared for flooded through her. "I was beginning to think you weren't coming," she said.

"Steve dropped by as I was about to leave. He's upset because Mum's staying another week at her retreat."

"You should have brought him with you."

"Nah, he's an old grump when he's like this." Jack touched her shoulder and leaned in to brush her cheek with his lips. He smelled fresh from the shower, with just a hint of aftershave. "If he hadn't showed up I would have come early to help you cook."

Thank God for Steve. "Why, so you could say it was all your doing?" Her skin tingled from the imprint of his mouth. "Men are so arrogant."

"You wouldn't have gotten that tire changed without me."

"*I* changed that tire." She led the way into the house.

"What's for dinner?" he said, following. "It smells delicious."

"Oh, just a little thing I whipped up," she said airily. "Grilled quail with Puy lentils and...a few odds and ends."

"Sounds ambitious. Just your style."

She threw him a glance over her shoulder. "Yes, it is."

Sienna ushered him into the lounge room. Jack already knew Peter, so she introduced him to Martin and Glyneth and Rex, then left them chatting while she went around and topped up aperitif glasses with more sherry. She checked her watch as she hurried back to the kitchen, mentally ticking off her schedule. She'd give Jack five more minutes to settle in, then she'd bring out the sparkling wine and the oysters. At the same time she would put the quail on to heat through. Half an hour for the appetizers, then she'd call everyone to the dining room for the main course. As long as she didn't forget to breathe everything would be okay.

She was juggling the platter of raw oysters and another bottle of sparkling wine under her arm when Jack came up behind her. "Oh! You scared me."

"Oysters, huh?" He shot her a sly sideways grin. And took the wine bottle from her.

"I saw Paul down at the shops today," she said, ignoring the innuendo. "He got a job with the municipal council."

"Excellent." Jack picked an oyster on a half shell from the tray. "What did you dress these with?"

Uh-oh. Sienna studied the oyster in its pool of clear liquid flecked with tiny pieces of red. One taste and Jack would be able to identify the ingredients. "You have to guess."

He tilted his head back and slipped the oyster into his mouth, savoring the morsel before swallowing. "Lime and red chili."

"Bingo!" She took one and tossed it down. "Not bad, if I do say so myself."

"Where'd you get the recipe?" Jack asked, reaching for another.

"I...I made it up. I mean, you can't get much simpler than lime juice and chili." She was such a bad liar; she felt sure her conscience showed in her pink cheeks and shifty eyes.

"Lime juice and chili, my favorite. Good work, Dr. Maxwell." His sexy smile left her feeling guilty and gooey at the same time.

Everything was going swimmingly when they rejoined the others. The food was superb, the wine plentiful and the conversation buzzing. Glyneth and Rex were mixing easily with Renita and Martin. Peter and Lexie had found her collection of vintage vinyl and put a Billie Holiday record on the stereo.

"You own a turntable. I'm impressed," Jack said.

With all the available seating taken, Sienna and Jack had to stand. She was backed up against the bookshelf with Jack forced inside her personal space by the cramped quarters. Every time she moved, she brushed his arm or his hip, feeling the heat of his body through his thin pullover and black denim jeans.

"It belonged to my aunt," she explained. "When she moved out of her house into an apartment she was throwing things out. I rescued the record player and all her albums."

"I'll bring over my old swing records sometime." His gaze drifted to her lips, to her breasts and back to her eyes. "I love to…dance."

Oh. My. God. One more second of those hot dark eyes and she was going to spontaneously combust.

Beep. Beep. Beep.

"Sienna, is that a timer going off?" Renita asked.

"The quail!" She brushed past Jack, pressing him back with a hand on his chest. "Excuse me."

"Want some help?" he asked.

"I've got it." If there was any more burned poultry in her oven she wanted to deal with it on her own. "Dinner should be ready in a few minutes."

She pulled the tray of grilled quail from the oven, set it on the counter and tugged off an oven mitt to test the firmness of one golden-brown breast. Done to perfection. With the quail plated on warmed china she then got the side dishes set out, candles lit and bottles of wine placed at intervals down the damask-draped table. When the table was perfect she called her guests.

Sienna had given some thought to the seating arrangement, but no one noticed her place cards and sat wherever they felt like it. Looking at the ring of glowing congenial faces, she decided she didn't care. She was surrounded by friends, new and old. Nothing else seemed important.

Until Glyneth took a bite of her quail and went into raptures. "Oh, my God, Sienna! Summerside really has changed you. No offense, but you've never made anything half this good in your life."

Jack glanced at Sienna with mild curiosity.

"Thanks, Glyneth." Sienna cut into the quail breast. It melted in her mouth. Wow, it really was tasty. Glyneth was right; she could never have pulled this off. Yet. Give her time; she would learn.

"Mmm. You have to give me the recipe," Renita said.

One by one, around the table, her guests complimented the meal lavishly. Guilt speared her with every tribute, but it was too late to confess now. If she made it through tonight without being caught, she resolved to take a cooking class.

Jack voiced his approval with the others, but mostly he was quiet.

And then Martin said, "I bought quail similar to this from the Instant Gourmet in the village last week."

Sienna froze, her fork halfway to her mouth. "You did?"

"Yours is much better, though."

Sienna could barely choke down the morsel on her fork. Perspiration dampened her hairline. What had she done? She wished a trapdoor would open beneath her chair and swallow her up, phony dinner and all. She wished she could laugh it off and confess the truth. Instead she smiled tightly and said, "Thank you. More lentils?"

"Where do you get these Puy lentils?" Lexie asked. "I haven't been able to find them in Summerside."

"I…l-let me see," Sienna stammered. Her throat closed up at the thought of uttering another lie. "I can't remember."

"Bromptons Deli in Mornington carries them," Jack said. "Maybe that's where you got them. Or else some place in the city?"

"M-Mornington."

"I'll have to get some," Lexie said. "This is a lot like the lentil dish you make, Jack. I *love* that."

Sienna had to grip the seat of her chair so as not to squirm like a six-year-old. She was a grown woman, a doctor and a respected member of the community. How had she gotten herself into this situation? Her own stupid pride, that's how.

"Something like it," Jack agreed. "Rex, is that your '67 Jaguar out front?"

"It is." Rex beamed. Without further prompting he launched into a tale of how much trouble he had getting parts.

Sienna breathed out slowly and unclenched her fists in her lap. Gradually she relaxed enough to ask Glyneth how things were at City Hospital, where Glyneth was head nurse. She told her friend about Erica, and about Oliver's canceled trip and his lip piercing. Glyneth in turn told her about the new registrar who was a pain in the butt, Rex's mother, who was staying with them for all of December, and their fifteen-year-old daughter's first boyfriend.

When everyone was finished eating Sienna removed the dinner plates and brought out goblets of tiramisu. "Who wants coffee and who wants tea?"

She had both ready to go, so it was merely a matter of filling cups and ferrying sugar and cream to the table.

"You're so organized," Lexie said. "I don't know how you do it. Especially with all the food preparation. It was absolutely perfect."

"Please, it was nothing." She really wished the praise would stop. She wasn't perfect; she was deceitful.

Jack dug in to his tiramisu. "This is seriously good. You must have spent days cooking."

Her misery was complete. He believed in her, trusted her, and she'd lied to him.

It was well past midnight before Sienna hugged Glyneth and Rex goodbye at the door. Renita, Martin, Lexie and Peter had left half an hour earlier.

"Come and visit us," Glyneth said. "You, too, Jack."

"You bet." Jack followed Rex off the veranda. "I'll take a closer look at the Jag before you go."

While Jack and Rex went to examine the car, Sienna was grateful for a private moment with Glyneth. "What should I do about Erica? Anthony wants me to go see her."

"Why, so he can rub your nose in it?" Glyneth said. "I'm sorry she's not well, but it's asking too much from you."

"She was my friend."

"Until she stole your husband. You don't owe her anything." Glyneth gave her another hug. "Forget about them. Things seem to have worked out well for you in Summerside. Jack is a keeper."

"I'm telling you, we're not together." And if he ever found out what she'd done tonight, he wouldn't respect her.

Sienna waved and walked back up the path into the house. The sound of clinking glass coming from the garage hurried her through the hall. Jack was putting the wine bottles into the recycling bin. Oh, no. There was no way he could have missed seeing the Instant Gourmet wrappings.

Jack came into the kitchen from the brightly lit garage. His eyes met hers, knocking the wind out of her. *He knew.*

His lowered eyebrows and down-turned mouth made her realize just how congenial his usual expression was. Now he just looked...angry. Sienna felt the rich tiramisu rise in her stomach. "You caught me red-handed. Jack, I lied. I'm sorry."

To her surprise, he burst out laughing. "I knew the moment you made me guess about the dressing for the oysters. You should have seen your face when you tried to come up with an answer."

"What? You think this is funny? I lied to you, to everyone." She plunged her hands into her hair, wishing she could pull it over her face and hide. "This is the most embarrassing moment of my life."

Sobering, Jack leaned against the counter, elbows angled back. "Why did you do it?"

"I wanted to impress you with my cooking. You're so good yourself and I know you set a lot of store by dinner parties…" She trailed off. It was pointless to go on.

"No, you did it because you're an overachiever. And possibly because you wanted to show me up, to prove a person could do anything they set their mind to. If you could pull off a gourmet meal, I could build a perfect GPS, run the Men's Shed, become prime minister, fly to the moon…"

"Okay, just stop."

"Don't you get it?" he continued. "The food is secondary. The whole point of a dinner party is the *company*. Do you really think I'm such a…a shallow person as to care about whether the lentils come from France or bloody Timbuktu? I wouldn't care if you opened a tin of beans. I'd eat three-day-old leftovers. I'd eat two-minute noodles. I'd eat frickin' stale crackers if—"

"If what?"

He sucked in a breath and then let it out in a gust. "And by the way, I'm friends with the owner of Instant Gourmet."

She groaned. "Of course you are. You know everyone in town. How did I ever think I could get away with it?"

"That's my lentil recipe."

She buried her face in her hands. "I can't look you in the eye," she said, her voice muffled. "Just walk away and leave me to fall on my chef's knife."

He chuckled. "I think it's cute that you wanted to impress me."

"I don't want to be cute. I want to be perfect."

"Perfection isn't top of my list of desirable qualities in a woman." Then he was pulling her hands away from her face and brushing back her hair. "You're so smart and efficient, if you didn't have some faults you'd be intimidating."

"I don't have faults—just endearing idiosyncrasies."

"You have sexy breasts and a sweet little ass." He dipped his head and pulled her chin up. "And you're driving me crazy with wanting you."

He kissed her.

This isn't supposed to happen.

Yet Sienna found herself running her hands up his chest and across his broad shoulders. Her eyes fluttered closed under the onslaught of Jack's mouth. And his hands. *Oh, his hands.* Cupping her face, outlining the shape of her hips, her waist, her breasts. Sliding beneath her blouse, so hot she could swear she heard her skin sizzle.

With difficulty she pushed away from him.

"What's wrong?" His breath gusted against her neck, making her shiver.

"This isn't a good idea."

"You're right. It's the dumbest idea I've ever had."

"Then you should go."

"No, I should stay."

God help her, she wanted him to. He was making her crazy, too. She could never be with a man like Jack. But she couldn't stop thinking about him, night and day.

Sienna swallowed hard against her panic. How many years had it been since she'd been with a new man? Sixteen, seventeen?

"Okay, then," she said. "I'll show you my bedroom."

"Forget the bedroom," he said, his voice husky. "We'll do it right here."

CHAPTER THIRTEEN

"WHAT? WAIT—" Before she could speak another word he had his mouth on hers again, kissing her hungrily. This wasn't the way… She hadn't had time to prepare…

He backed her against the counter. Sandwiched between the cabinet and his hips, she felt heat curl through her. Jack broke the kiss and pulled her blouse over her head, her hair tickling her bare shoulders. He tossed her blouse over the bar stool on the other side of the counter and started to unbutton his shirt.

Sienna swallowed hard. His body was so taut and strong. Anthony had never been this fit. He shrugged out of his shirt, favoring his injured arm. Soon he would be naked. Then she would be naked. And they were going to have sex. In the kitchen. She nervously frayed the ends of a long strand of her hair. She'd come to Summerside looking for friends, not a lover. She needed time to get over Anthony, to reconnect with Oliver, to find herself, too.

"I have scented candles in the bedroom," she said, stalling. "A king-size mattress—"

"I don't need scented candles." He plunged his hands in her hair and tugged her forward, lowering his face to her neck. "Mmm. Pineapple." He nipped and licked his way down her neck. "Will Oliver be coming home soon?"

"He's staying overnight at Jason's."

Jack unhooked her bra and tossed it away. It landed half in the fruit bowl, one cup over a grapefruit.

"Sex doesn't belong in the *kitchen,*" she murmured. "I want this to be perfect."

"Sex doesn't have to be perfect. It belongs anywhere two people want to do it." He reached over and flicked off the light switch, leaving only the light over the stove.

He pulled her arms up around his neck, pressing her bare breasts against his chest.

Heat pooled in her belly and between her legs. With a sigh, she softened against his body. Her mind ceased its frenzied spinning and she focused only on the sensation of being in his arms.

His hands skimmed her hips, found her zipper and slid it down. Her skirt dropped around her ankles, trapping her in its folds. Then his hand dipped inside her lace panties, his work-roughened fingertips an erotic contrast to her slippery softness. Her knees sagged and she clung to him as he deepened the kiss.

She slid a hand down his chest and over his belly to open the snap on his jeans. Peeling them down, she saw that his black boxers were bulging. He had the tightest butt she'd ever curled her fingers around. Jack lowered his head to draw a taut nipple into his mouth and Sienna moaned softly. Their breathing was short and shallow, audible. She pressed her hips against his, trying to get as close as possible.

She gave a whoop as, without warning, he lifted her

onto the edge of the counter. Nudging her knees apart, he stepped between them while he alternately licked and sucked her nipples until she felt a sensual ache in her groin.

"Condom," she managed to whisper.

"I've got one," he said, fishing it out of his pocket.

It took him only a moment to get it on, and then he sank into her. She closed her legs around his hips. And then he started to move inside her and she gripped him tightly, her eyes glazed. The fruit bowl vibrated with every pump of his hips; her bra slipped off and fell onto the floor.

Clinging to his shoulders, Sienna arched her back, Jack held her in arms of iron, the tendons in his neck straining. Her muscles tightened and with a shuddering cry she held on to him as wave after wave convulsed her body. Triggered by her climax, Jack gave one last thrust. His body went rigid and he called her name.

Her heart still thundering in her ears, she collapsed her head on his shoulder. She'd needed this so badly, needed to just let go. It seemed to her she'd held herself in check ever since she'd made the decision to leave Anthony. Maybe even before that, when she'd agreed to marry him.

Maybe her whole life.

SOMETHING TICKLED Jack's nose, pulling him out of sleep. Eyes closed, he batted the thing away, scratched his bare chest and nuzzled deeper into the pillow. There it was again. He sneezed, his eyes still determinedly scrunched shut, his brain foggy. He knew it was Sunday morning, the only day he slept in. Dimly he wondered if Bogie had jumped onto his bed.

Then he heard a giggle.

His eyes snapped open. Sienna was leaning over him, wavy red hair spilling over her breasts. She was tickling his face with the tip of one long strand. Her gray-green eyes sparkled and her mouth curved deliciously behind her fingers as she tried to contain her laughter.

Jack came fully awake to find himself adrift in shell-pink-and-lavender linen that popped against slate-blue walls. “I never figured you for a pastel person.”

“There’s a lot you don’t know about me.” She kissed him lightly, then lay on her side, facing him on her pillow.

Her nose was slightly crooked and her chin too pointed to balance her wide-set eyes. In the morning light she looked like a flawed angel. “I know you’re beautiful.”

“How’s your shoulder?” she asked, her cheeks pink. “We got pretty acrobatic, even after we moved to the bedroom.”

“My shoulder’s fine.” It was a bit sore, but he didn’t want to talk about that. He rolled onto his back and pulled her into his arms, her head on his chest, her body tucked against his side, small and snug. The first year after Leanne died, he’d slept with a dozen women. The next year the number halved. He hadn’t formed a relationship with any of those women. He’d wanted meaningless sex—until he’d realized how empty that made him feel. This year there’d been no one.

“Do you want breakfast?” Sienna asked, rubbing lazy circles on his chest. She rolled onto her back and stretched her arms wide. "I'm *starving*. Coffee and toast okay?"

"Or you could run down to Instant Gourmet and get two orders of eggs Benedict," he murmured lazily.

She batted him with a pillow, forcing him awake. "You're never going to let me live that down, are you?"

"I made love with a woman who doesn't cook," Jack said to the ceiling. "I can't believe it."

"Stay there. I'll be right back." She bounded out of bed, her thick unruly hair swinging.

Jack was enjoying the sight of her nakedness, especially the sweet curve of her hips, but she pulled on a blue silk dressing gown, flipped her hair outside the collar and tied it tight. While she was gone he must have dozed again, because the next thing he knew she was bringing in a tray bearing steaming coffee and a plate of slightly burned toast. He struggled to a sitting position.

"I know it's not much nourishment for a man," she said, placing the tray on his lap while she climbed back into bed. "I was so traumatized by dinner party preparations I didn't buy any regular groceries."

"Next time we'll stay at my house and *I* will cook breakfast," he said, reaching for a mug.

"Next time?" She gave him a sidelong glance over a triangle of toast.

"Sure," he said cautiously. "Why not?" Then because she didn't answer right away, he filled the silence with the thing he'd been mulling over since he'd talked to Steve last night before the dinner party. "I've decided to start up the Men's Shed again."

She put down her toast. “That’s wonderful. When did you decide this?”

“Yesterday. Seeing my dad, I realized how much he needs the Shed. And, well, I enjoyed having a purpose to my day.” Jack glanced away, aware of the huge admission he’d just made, praying she didn’t make a big deal of it.

“I’m so happy,” she enthused. “For Steve, for the guys, for *you.* This is fantastic.” She punched him lightly on his good shoulder. “See, it wasn’t so hard. Your old life wasn’t working anymore, so you changed. Once you get the guys busy on a project, you can fix your GPS.”

Jack felt himself go cold. She thought *she’d* changed him. It was easy to make a suggestion—just start up a Men’s Shed, Jack, just invent a GPS—and another thing entirely to make it happen. If he mentioned that he was already working on the GPS, she’d be certain she had a hand in it. “What if I don’t want to?”

What if he couldn’t?

Her eyes widened as she realized her mistake. “I didn’t mean you *had* to.”

“I hope not.” If not the GPS, it would be something else. He had his life sorted out. He didn’t need to live up to her expectations.

Jack tried to go back to his breakfast, but he couldn’t relax. The lavender sheet was tucked under his butt, trapping him in place, and there were crumbs in his chest hair. The silence between him and Sienna wasn’t comfortable. Maybe breakfast in bed was just a bit too cozy, too soon. He set his half-finished coffee on the side table. "I'd better get home and let Bogie out. He'll be bursting."

"Are you sure?" She bit her lip. "I thought we could go for a walk later."

"I was going to go running." He pushed the covers back and yanked the sheet free so he could swing his legs out.

"I could run with you." When he didn't reply she added, "Or not. Never mind. Olly will be home soon. I should spend time with him today." She glanced at the clock and feigned surprise. "Wow, I had no idea it was that late."

Jack started to pull on his clothes. There was a hard lump in his throat. He couldn't leave her like this. "What about a movie later this week?"

"Sure! Thursday?"

"Ye— No, I promised Renita I'd go to an investment talk with her." Renita would let him off if he asked, but that cold part of him didn't want to ask. "Friday?"

"Can't," Sienna said. "Bev, the receptionist at the clinic, invited me to her daughter's hen night."

"Okay." Jack scrubbed a hand through his hair. This was awful. He was crazy about this woman. He absolutely could not walk out and leave her feeling rejected. But for the life of him he couldn't seem to get back that warm fuzzy feeling. "I'll give you a call. We'll sort something out."

"You're mad at me for bringing up your GPS," she said flatly, her arms hanging at her sides.

"No, of course not." He pulled her into a hug and rested his chin on top of her head. "*Thank you* for a fantastic night. If I don't run into you beforehand we'll catch up for dinner at my place on Saturday." He looked down. Damn if her eyes weren't glistening.

"Perfect." She blinked, then forced a smile. "Saturday."

SIENNA SLAPPED SLICED chicken and lettuce on a whole-wheat roll for Oliver's school lunch. She hadn't slept well in two days and was grumpy and out of sorts, with a nagging headache that wouldn't go away. She hadn't heard a peep from Jack since he'd left Sunday morning. A dozen times she'd thought about calling him, then had to ask herself, what for? He was busy. They'd established that they couldn't get together until Saturday. Wasn't that enough? Did she need reassurance that badly?

Saturday seemed very far away.

"Olly! Hurry or you'll be late for school."

Why had she asked Jack about his GPS? She knew it was a sore spot and she was pushing him. But honestly, why *wouldn't* he rework such an important project?

It'll be okay. I'll see him on Saturday.

And yet he hadn't changed and never would. Maybe he was right to pull back. When she saw him again, she would let him know that she'd had second thoughts, too.

Suddenly Saturday seemed way too close.

She wrapped the chicken sandwich in plastic and grabbed an apple from the fridge. "Olly!" she called more sharply than she'd intended.

"I'm here." Avoiding her gaze, he slunk around the corner and went to the pantry for cereal. "What's eating you?"

"Nothing," she said. "Your math test is today. Did you study?"

"Yeah. 'Course." He poured wheat flakes into a bowl.

When? she wondered. Not at Jason's, probably. Sunday night he'd watched TV. And last night when she'd gone into his room he was texting his friends.

She glanced at the clock. "I'm late for my rounds at the hospital. Look, I know you haven't been very happy lately, missing out on the ski trip, but you need to do well on this test. It's extremely important."

He grunted, head down as he continued to eat.

"If you blow it you won't be allowed to take advanced math next year, which you need to get into science at uni."

"I *know,* Mum," Oliver growled. "Just go."

SIENNA HAD JUST EXCISED a sebaceous cyst from a female patient's back and was preparing to stitch up the wound when Bev poked her head into the surgical room and motioned her over.

"The principal of Oliver's school, Andrea Dillard, is on the phone," Bev said. "I told her you were busy. She said it was important."

"Is Oliver injured?" Covering her anxiety with a mask of calm, Sienna popped the cyst into a container, to be analyzed at the lab.

"Nothing like that. She didn't say what the problem was. Shall I ask her to hold?"

"I can't talk right now. Tell her I'll call back in twenty minutes."

Sienna sutured the wound and applied a surgical

dressing, explaining the aftercare to her patient. All the while her mind was racing, wondering what was wrong. When she was finished and had answered all the patient's questions she walked down the hall to her office to call the principal.

Five minutes later she was on her way to the school.

Oliver was sitting in the principal's office, a scowl on his face, his hands clasped between his knees.

Andrea Dillard's smooth dark hair was pulled back and her narrow glasses were perched on the end of her long nose. Rising behind her desk, she shook Sienna's hand. "Please, sit down."

Sienna took a chair next to Oliver. She squeezed his shoulder and turned to Ms. Dillard. "What's this about?"

The principal pursed her narrow lips and looked over her glasses. "Oliver has been accused of cheating on his math exam."

Sienna's grip tightened on the wooden arms of her chair. She turned to Olly, trying but failing to keep the shock out of her voice. "Is this true?"

"No!" Oliver said. "Just because that dickhead Harris—"

"Oliver!" Sienna leaned forward and rested one hand on Ms. Dillard's desk. "What exactly happened?"

"Robert Harris, a top student, was away for the original exam," the woman explained. "The two boys took it together. Robert claims he saw Oliver glancing over at his exam paper."

"So it's his word against Olly's." Sienna sat back,

her hands twisting together in her lap. "What does the teacher say? Did he see Oliver cheat?"

"He observed Oliver looking around the room—"

"I was thinking," Oliver blurted out.

"Please do not interrupt," Andrea said. She removed an exam paper from a folder on her desk and handed it to Sienna. "Your son got ninety-eight percent on the test, exactly the same as the other boy."

Sienna flipped through the stapled sheets of typed questions and handwritten answers. The paper trembled in her hands as she noted that there was very little working out of problems on the page. "That doesn't prove Oliver cheated. He's a smart boy. The identical scores could be a coincidence. Some other kids must have got a high grade."

"A couple of students did." The principal took off her glasses and let them hang on the beaded chain around her neck. "But Oliver's grades this term have been a C average. Unless he's been studying extrahard it's difficult to account for such a marked improvement."

"Oliver, what do you have to say?" Sienna asked.

"I didn't cheat." His shoulders were hunched up around his ears, his long legs bent at awkward angles to avoid bumping his knees on the principal's desk.

"I don't have to tell you this is serious business, Dr. Maxwell," Ms. Dillard said severely. "Cheating renders Oliver's mark void and excludes him from the advanced math class next year."

The bottom dropped out of Sienna's stomach. For a moment she was frozen to her chair, then she surged to her feet. "You have no actual proof," she protested. "Can't he take the exam again?"

"I'm afraid not. This was already a makeup test. I understand he missed the first one due to truancy." The phone rang and she answered it. "All right." She hung up and rose. "Excuse me a moment. I'll be right back."

When she'd left the office, Sienna turned to Oliver. "You know what this means—no medical school. You'll never be a doctor after this."

In sullen silence he fiddled with the stud in his lip.

Sienna wanted to slap his hand away, but she reined in her anger, taking a deep breath to regain the calm she needed. "Don't you have anything to say for yourself?"

"Medical school was your dream for me, not mine. I didn't want to take the stupid test in the first place." Oliver crossed his arms over his chest and fixed his gaze on the floor.

Sienna studied him with a stab of guilt. She'd been pressuring him for weeks. Maybe he'd cracked under the strain. Glancing at the door to make sure it was shut, she said in a softer voice, "I know what it's like to feel expected to perform. Everyone makes mistakes. I won't think less of you if you just tell me the truth."

Olly's swift glance revealed the depth of his hurt and betrayal. "You don't believe me?"

"I believe you're *capable* of passing the test if you'd studied."

"I didn't need to study. The questions were easy."

"That boy saw you looking at his paper."

"He's an idiot!" Oliver got to his feet, agitated.

"Your teacher saw you looking around."

"I finished early. I was bored."

"There was no working out of the answers on your test."

"I did them in my head!"

"Keep your voice down." Sienna glanced at the closed door again. "This is serious. Ms. Dillard will be back any minute."

But Oliver was too worked up. "I tried because *you* wanted it so badly. But when I get a high mark, you don't believe I did it without cheating." He tried to pace, but two long strides took him to the window overlooking the central courtyard where students were having lunch.

"Oliver, listen to me." Sienna leaned forward, resting her forearms on her knees, hands clasped. "I've never told anyone this..." She sucked in a breath. "*I* cheated on a test once. In grade three."

"You cheated? No way."

"It's true." Her head dropped. At eight years old, the anxiety of knowing she wasn't going to get a perfect score when she *always* got one hundred percent had forced her to take desperate measures.

"When I realized I didn't know an answer I looked at another girl's paper." Sienna twisted her fingers together, flooded even now with guilt and remorse. "The girl told the teacher. My mother and father came down to the school. I'd always been so good and so smart that my parents refused to believe I would cheat. I was afraid of letting them down, so I lied." Sienna shook her head, feeling her heavy hair sway. "The girl who accused me got in trouble instead. I felt awful. I've never been able to forget it. Needless to say, I never cheated again."

But she'd lied about dinner.

"So because *you're* a cheater you think *I* am, too?" Oliver said disdainfully.

Sienna's head came up. "I don't want you to fall into that trap. Or think you have to lie so I'll be proud of you."

"No, I just have to do exactly what you want." Oliver's lip curled in a sneer. "You always pretend you're so perfect, but you cheated. Stop acting like you're better than me—and don't keep telling me what to do!"

Sienna's cheeks burned as she gazed straight ahead. She *was* a liar and a cheat. Oliver would never respect her again. Swallowing, she straightened her shoulders. Today wasn't about her. She had to stop Oliver from making a huge mistake.

"If you tell Ms. Dillard the truth she might reconsider."

"I did tell the truth," Oliver raged. "I don't want to take it again. I don't want to go to uni. I don't want to be a doctor."

"Oliver, control yourself."

All of a sudden he calmed down. "Okay, I'll 'control' myself." He strode past her to the door and opened it. Students were in the corridor between classes. "As soon as I turn sixteen I'm going to quit school."

Sienna sprang to her feet, hands clenched. "I forbid you!"

"You can't stop me." Then he melted into the passing tide of chattering teens.

THE WORKSHOP DOOR OPENED and Jack glanced up from the laptop he'd set up on the workbench, surprised to see

Oliver in the middle of a school day. He quickly saved his program. "Hey, Olly. What's up?"

"Nothin'." His hands were jammed into his front pockets.

"Shouldn't you be in school?"

Oliver shuffled his oversize feet, not looking him in the eye. "Got out early."

"Does your mother know where you are?"

"No!" Oliver flared, his head coming up, his pimples standing out bright red.

"Whoa. What's the problem?" Jack unplugged the soldering iron and perched on a stool. "Sit down and tell me about it."

Oliver was too worked up to sit. He paced the big open space between the ultralight aircraft and the work-bench, clenching and unclenching his fists. "I'm going to quit school when I'm sixteen. I want to get an apprenticeship." He turned suddenly. "Can I train with you?"

"I'd happily teach you what I know, Olly. But I don't have a business for you to learn. If you're going to do this, you need to do it right and get hired on at a big company. Besides, your mother would have my hide if I said yes."

Oliver's chin jutted out. "I'm making my own decisions now. I could start with you, couldn't I?"

"Tell me what happened," Jack said. The boy had more crises than the Middle East.

Olly flung himself into a straight-back wooden chair, making the legs scrape across the concrete. "Mum doesn't believe I didn't cheat on a test at school."

Seeing the hurt on Oliver's young face, Jack felt his

own sense of outrage. How could Sienna not trust her own son? "*I* believe you."

"Then tell her. She'll listen to *you*."

Outside a car door slammed. Seconds later Sienna marched in, her back stiff and her face white. "Hello, Jack," she said, barely glancing at him. "I thought I'd find you here," she said to her son. "Go get in the car."

"No," Oliver said.

Sienna's grip tightened on the shoulder strap of her purse, but she clearly fought to stay calm. "I've spoken to your father. Whether you cheated or not is immaterial. The point is, you're falling behind in school and going off the rails in other ways. Which means I'm… I'm failing you." Sucking in a breath, she continued. "Anthony and I have agreed. You're going to go live with him and Erica until you finish grade twelve."

"But…" Oliver's mouth fell open.

"There is no discussion," she said. "You will not be quitting school. You will not be doing an apprenticeship."

She pointed to the door. Shell-shocked and speechless, Oliver stumbled out, dragging his feet.

Sienna started after him. Jack caught her by the arm. "Maybe this is none of my business—"

"You're right, it's not," she snapped.

"But I care about Olly. He told me what happened. Trust him, back him up."

"Olly knows I love him even if he makes a mistake. That's what's important." Sienna tugged her arm away from Jack.

"Remember I said being perfect wasn't at the top of

my list of desirable qualities? *Loyalty* is." Jack shook his head. "If you love someone you stick by them. Let the math test go. Let him choose the profession he wants to go into."

"He doesn't have to do medicine. But he has to finish school and go to university." She looked Jack straight in the eye. "He has the brains—he shouldn't waste them."

Anger surged through Jack. "Or what, he's not good enough for you?"

"He's my son."

"Stop trying to control him." Jack was nose-to-nose with her now, his blood up, and he was glad they were finally having this out. "Stop trying to fulfill your own ambitions through him. You want so badly to be perfect but you're not, so you try to make everyone around you live up to your impossible standards."

She jerked as though he'd slapped her. Which meant he'd touched a very sore nerve. "Love Olly for who he is," Jack urged. "Not for who *you* want him to be."

"I do love Olly for who he is." Tears sprang to her eyes. "That's why I want him to reach his full potential."

"*Your* definition of his potential."

She dashed away the tears on her cheeks. "I have to do what I think is best for Oliver. If you don't agree, that's too bad."

"Then there's nothing more to be said."

"On the contrary. I have more to say." She stabbed a finger at him. "*You're* no one to give my son career advice. You feel guilty because your GPS failed and your wife died. I'm sorry about Leanne. Really sorry.

But you can't move on because you're too busy punishing yourself. You say you live for pleasure? Ha! If that was true you'd be flying."

She started to walk away, then spun around. "Yes, success is important to me. But I don't measure success by how much a person achieves. I measure it by how hard they try. And *you're* not trying hard enough. As far as I can see, you're not trying at all. Maybe I place too many expectations on myself and others, but you have too few."

Without another word she strode back to her car. The door slammed, the engine revved and gravel spurted from beneath her tires as she drove off.

Jack kicked a fallen offcut across the concrete floor.

"Good riddance."

The words sounded hollow.

CHAPTER FOURTEEN

"ARE YOU READY TO GO?" Sienna poked her head inside Oliver's bedroom. He was lying on his bed surrounded by piles of unpacked clothes, texting on his mobile phone. "Your father's expecting you. We're going to be late."

"I have to tell Jason I'm leaving," Olly said, his thumbs continuing to fly over the keys.

The landline rang in the kitchen. "Hurry," Sienna said, and went to answer the phone. It was her mother, Barbara. Sienna was unable to hide her surprise. Her mother was usually too busy at the Mayo Clinic to call except on birthdays or at Christmas. Instinctively Sienna stood straighter, glancing at her reflection in the windows to see if her hair was neat. "How's Dad? Nothing's wrong, is there?"

"Everything's fine," Barbara said. "I got your email that you were moving. Sorry I haven't got back to you before now. Where is Summerside? Is it a long commute to City Hospital?"

"I quit the hospital. I'm head of a general practice clinic now."

"What? You didn't tell me that."

"I'm telling you now."

"Really, Sienna." Disapproval tinged her mother's

voice. "If you'd stuck it out at the hospital another five years or so you could have been head of orthopedics."

Sienna pressed two fingers to her temple. No matter what she did, or how well she did it, it was never enough. "I made the move for Olly's sake." Tears burned the backs of her eyes. He was upstairs, packing to leave the place she'd moved to for him.

"How *is* Oliver? I hope you didn't take him out of Wesley College and enroll him in a local public school."

"The train line runs right past the Wesley." Sienna could just imagine what her mother would say about Olly's plan to drop out of school entirely. But why give any more information than she had to? Once Oliver was living at Anthony's, he would go back to his old private school, temporarily at least.

"Are you coming back to Australia for Christmas?" Sienna asked. "I have plenty of room, and Summerside is lovely in summer."

"I'd like to, but we may have to work through the holiday," Barbara said. "I'll let you know. I'd better go. Your father sends his love."

"Is he there?" Sienna asked. "Can I talk to him?"

"We're on our way out the door. Maybe next time."

Sienna suppressed a sigh. "I'm in a rush, too. Bye, Mum."

In the car Oliver sat in stony silence for the first half hour. Then he said, "Erica's sick and she's having a baby. She won't want me there."

"Erica's fine with whatever your father wants. Your dad wants you with him. He feels bad about canceling the ski trip." It felt as if she was reciting something in a book—not quite real.

"*You* want me gone."

"No, I—" Sienna stopped. No more lies. No more pretending. "I just think you need to take a step back, think about who you are and where you're going. You didn't have crazy ideas about quitting school when you were living in the city and attending Wesley College."

"Robotics isn't a crazy idea. Maybe I'm just finding out who I am because I'm older now."

Sienna didn't want their last conversation for a while to be an argument, so she let a beat go by and then changed the subject. "It'll be fun when the baby comes home."

"Oh, yeah, a laugh a minute." Oliver turned and gazed out his side window.

Sienna glanced at his profile—shut down—then at the blue waters of the bay, visible between the town houses flashing by on the beach side of the highway. She wondered if Jack was kayaking today or if he was getting the Men's Shed rolling.

Tears blurred her vision, and the car in front of theirs smeared into red and silver streaks. Furiously she blinked them away. She was only trying to do what was right for her son. Someday he would realize that. It didn't matter what Jack thought anymore.

Oliver seemed as lost in his own thoughts as she was and the miles ticked away until she was pulling up in front of Anthony's apartment building. She rang his mobile. "We're here. Could you come down and give us a hand with Oliver's bags?"

"I'm at the hospital." Anthony sounded harried.

"Did something come up?" Sienna glanced at Olly, afraid he'd take this as a sign his dad wasn't interested in him.

"Sorry, I should have called. Erica was induced this afternoon. She had the baby."

"Is she all right? Is the baby okay?" At the thought of a preemie her maternal instincts won out over jealousy.

"Erica's doing fine, considering. Tamara's in a humidicrib, but she's breathing on her own." His voice was filled with pride. "Why don't you and Oliver come here? You can see Erica and the baby, then Olly can go home with me."

"Uh..." Excuses ran through her mind. But her last encounter with Jack had left her feeling mean-spirited. She would like to think she was capable of more generosity. "We'll be there shortly."

"Wonderful." The genuine pleasure in Anthony's voice made her glad she'd said yes. When all was said and done he was still the father of her child.

Twenty minutes later, standing outside Erica's hospital room, Sienna felt her doubts come rushing back. She wasn't sure she could face the woman who'd betrayed her friendship. If she couldn't be sincerely happy for Erica she had no business being here.

"Are we just going to stand out here in the hall?" Oliver asked, shuffling in his size-twelve sneakers. "I want to get this over with."

"You go in," Sienna said. "I'm going to the nursery."

Anthony poked his head out the door. "I thought I heard your voices." He gave Sienna a peck on the cheek and Oliver a quick hug. Then he was ushering them inside the ward before Sienna could utter a word of protest. "Look who's here, Erica."

"I really can't stay—" Sienna broke off.

Erica's eyes were closed, her face puffy with edema. Dark skin below her eyes gave her a bruised appearance. She was hooked up to an IV and a catheter. An oxygen monitor was clipped to her right index finger. Her eyelids fluttered open and she smiled weakly. "Thanks for coming."

Sienna managed to nod. She picked Erica's chart off the end of the bed and scanned it, giving herself time to adjust. Erica's blood pressure was elevated and there was protein in her urine. She was still very ill.

"Say hello, Oliver," Anthony prompted.

Oliver grunted something that sounded like a greeting, then retreated to a chair beside the window.

Sienna approached the bed, not sure what to say.

"Anthony, why don't you take Oliver to the nursery to see Tamara?" Erica suggested.

Panic fluttered through Sienna as Anthony and Oliver left the room. The silence between Sienna and Erica grew and grew, until Sienna felt crushed by the weight of everything they weren't saying.

"I didn't mean for it to happen," Erica said at last. "Anthony and I."

"Don't talk about that now," Sienna said quickly, not wanting to talk about it *ever.* "You're ill."

"I need to say it. We were friends once and I owe you that much." Erica paused to catch her breath. "If I die—"

"You're not going to die," Sienna said automatically, though she knew it was a possibility. As a doctor she was used to dealing with reality. But suddenly it was terrifying to think that Erica, a new mother, could actually pass away.

She lowered herself into the chair beside the bed, twisting her hands together. "Go on if you want to."

"There's nothing to say, really. I'm just sorry."

"Sorry you broke up my marriage?" Sienna heard the words come from her lips, harsh and unforgiving. How was it possible for compassion to exist alongside anger?

"At first we just talked. He wasn't happy."

"So what if he was unhappy?" Sienna demanded fiercely. "You could have told him to go home and sort things out with his wife. If he was that unhappy he should have talked to *me*."

Erica's gaze sharpened. "He said he tried. You were never available."

"That's not true," Sienna shot back.

"Wasn't it?" Erica asked, unwavering.

Sienna forced herself to try to see the past objectively. *Had* Anthony tried to talk about their relationship? She thought of all her late nights on duty, of how she'd insisted on Oliver accompanying them everywhere, of the many times she'd fallen into bed too exhausted for anything but sleep. She had to admit she'd avoided spending time alone with Anthony. Had she been so used to papering over the cracks in her marriage that she hadn't seen how deep they'd become?

"Sienna?" Erica said.

Sienna gazed at the woman straddling the razor's edge between life and death. She could play the aggrieved first wife or she could be honest with herself and Erica.

"I didn't love him," Sienna admitted. "Not even at first. I liked him a lot. But I didn't love him. I got pregnant in med school. We married because in my family daughters didn't become single mothers." It was so simple, yet so huge. How was it possible she'd never admitted it to herself before? How had Anthony lived with that? "My whole marriage was a lie."

"I envied you so much," Erica said slowly. "A brilliant husband, a stellar career, a son. If that wasn't enough there was the fabulous apartment, trips to Europe, fine restaurants. You had the perfect life, the perfect marriage."

Perfect. There was that word again.

"I worked so many hours I didn't have time to enjoy anything." Sienna gazed at her palms wondering irrelevantly which was the life line and which the heart line.

"You went from success to success, while I was a childless screwup with a broken marriage and a crappy job."

"Now *I* have the broken marriage, a job my mother doesn't respect and my son hates me." Sienna gave Erica a humorless smile. "Funny, huh?"

Erica reached out. With all the tubes running into her hand she could touch Sienna's only with the tips of her fingers. "You're still *you.* And you're pretty exceptional, warts and all."

"But I'm not perfect." That sounded childish. But she *felt* like a child, petulant and spoiled. Also constrained and pressured. Sienna burst into tears.

"No one's perfect," Erica said quietly.

"I tried to be. What an idiot I was." She took a tissue from the box on Erica's bedside table and blew her nose. "Please don't tell me that you only had an affair with Anthony because you were envious of me. It would be so unfair to him if you don't love him, either."

"I love him," Erica said. "I didn't want him out of envy or to take something away from you."

"Good." Sienna balled up the tissue, dabbed her eyes and took a deep breath. "So, how are you feeling?"

"I'm so afraid," Erica whispered.

"You're going to be fine," Sienna said, automatically using her doctor's voice, confident and reassuring. "Your baby is receiving the best possible care—" Seeing Erica's eyes glaze over, she broke off. Erica had plenty of doctors; right now she needed a friend.

"It sucks, you being sick while Tamara is in neonatal intensive care," she said softly.

"I just want to go home with my baby."

"You will, in a few weeks." Sienna reached out and massaged warmth into Erica's cold fingers. "Anthony was great when Olly was born. He'll take good care of you and Tamara."

"Thank you." Erica clung to Sienna's hand. "Glyneth said you've settled in to Summerside. Nice friends, a new man?"

"Oh, well." Sienna wiped away her tears with the back of her hand. "I screwed up there, too."

"How do you mean?"

"It seems I pressure people with high expectations. I pushed him away. And this time…" She let out a deep sigh. "I really love the guy."

"Then you should let him know."

Sienna shook her head. "Too late."

"If he loves you, he'll forgive you."

"It's not just that. He doesn't let me in, not completely." Sienna wasn't sure how to explain, or if she even understood it herself. "He's got some emotional block about his wife's death. I've tried to talk to him."

"Maybe you should listen instead." Yawning, Erica closed her eyes. Her face was pale and drawn.

"I'm going to go," Sienna said. "You need to rest up for when you see your daughter later." She hesitated, then leaned through the wires and drips to touch Erica on the cheek. "Take care."

Erica's eyes fluttered open. "It's okay for Olly to stay with us. I hope I didn't hurt his feelings. I've been pretty anxious about the baby and everything."

"He's going through some teen stuff. He's okay," Sienna said. "But I'm not sure I want to let him go. I'll talk to Anthony."

She found him and Oliver at the neonatal intensive care unit, standing over a humidicrib. Her steps slowed. This was another milestone—Anthony's baby with another woman. Her friend Erica's baby, she reminded herself. Anthony and Oliver stepped aside as she approached.

She gazed into the Plexiglas crib. The infant was no bigger than Anthony's hand and wore only a tiny diaper and knit cap. Eye patches protected her vision from the fluorescent bilirubin lights. As Anthony had said, she was breathing on her own. But she had an umbilical catheter and a nasogastric tube inserted for feeding. An

IV needle dangled from her limp arm for administering medicine.

Life was so fragile. Yet so tenacious. Tamara's pulse, visible through translucent skin, beat away despite all the odds.

Her gaze shifted to *her* baby, Oliver. He was already moving out of her home. It was what she'd dreaded, yet *she'd* been the one to initiate it. How could she have been so wrong?

Sienna glanced at Anthony. "She looks like you."

Anthony's sudden smile lit his narrow face. "You think so?"

"I'm not sure that's a compliment, Dad," Oliver said. "She looks like a skinned rabbit."

"You should have seen yourself when you were born," Anthony replied. "When we get back home I'll show you some photos I've been saving for your twenty-first birthday party."

Oliver groaned, but he didn't look entirely displeased.

Amused, Sienna assessed father and son. "Do you get to hold her?" she asked Anthony.

"In the evening we have kangaroo care. Skin to skin," Anthony explained to Olly. "She's placed on my chest or Erica's to promote healing and bonding."

Oliver stared at the baby as if just now realizing how small she was. "Tamara *is* going to make it, isn't she?"

"She's a fighter," Anthony said, gazing at his daughter. "She'll make it."

"Olly, will you wait for me outside?" Sienna said. "I want to talk to your father." She waited until he'd left to say, "I've changed my mind. I want to take Oliver back to Summerside."

Anthony frowned. "Why?"

"For one thing, Erica and the baby will need all your attention in the next few months. Also, I should have given Olly the benefit of the doubt over the exam. I don't want him to think I'm getting rid of him. God knows, I'd miss him like crazy if he wasn't around."

"I miss him, too. I was looking forward to having him." Anthony thought a moment. "Erica's going to be in the hospital for a while yet. Why doesn't Olly stay with me over his two-week term break, then go back to you when school starts again?"

Sienna smiled. "That sounds like a plan."

"Are you okay?" Anthony asked, placing a hand on her shoulder. "You seem stressed."

"I've had a tough week," she admitted.

"You're too hard on yourself." Anthony's arm went around her in a quick hug. "You need to take care."

"Thanks." Sienna hugged him back, and to her surprise it felt natural. "Congratulations on your little girl. Make sure you take lots of time for her and Erica."

"Don't worry, I will."

Oliver was studying a vending machine in the waiting room when Sienna found him. She handed him some money from her wallet.

"Gee, thanks," he said, his eyes widening at the pair of twenties. "I only wanted a chocolate bar."

"It's spending money while you're at your father and Erica's place." Oliver started his automatic complaint, but Sienna cut him off. "You're only staying for the term break."

"Cool!" Oliver's face lit. "Thanks, Mum."

"I would have taken you straight home, but your dad really wants to spend time with you. You'll be coming back to Summerside to finish school." She gave him a stern look. "And by 'finish' I mean grade twelve. I'm sorry I doubted you," she went on quickly before he could speak. "I should have known you wouldn't lie."

Oliver's gaze dropped. His shoulders seemed to grow out of his ears.

"What is it?" she asked.

"Nothing."

"Oliver."

"Oh, all right," he mumbled. "I…I did cheat."

Sienna couldn't believe what she'd just heard. "I beg your pardon?"

"I'm sorry, okay?" he said with a return to defiance. "You were expecting me to ace the exam. I stared at those questions and I didn't know the answers. Robert was scribbling away like mad. I didn't know what else to do."

"So you're saying it's *my* fault?"

"You pressured me."

Sienna's mouth pressed tightly together and she spun away. It was true…up to a point. Turning back, she said, "You need to accept responsibility for your actions. As soon as you get back to Summerside, you're grounded again. And you'll have to tell your teacher and the principal."

"They won't let me sit the test again if I do that," Oliver said. "I won't be able to take advanced math."

"That's a price we'll both have to pay," Sienna said quietly.

Oliver hung his head. "I'm sorry I lied."

"Oh, Olly." Tears in her eyes, Sienna put her arms around him and hugged him tightly. "I'm sorry, too. We both should have done better."

"I'll finish grade twelve," Oliver said, his voice muffled in her hair. "But I don't want to be a doctor."

Sienna drew back and wiped her eyes. "How about a veterinarian?"

Oliver sighed with exaggerated patience. "No, Mum."

"Okay, okay. There's lots of time to decide."

WHERE IS STEVE? Jack glanced at his watch. His father had sounded eager to come back to the Shed and he'd promised he'd be there bright and early.

The radio was playing in the background, Ralph was operating an electric drill and Brett, one of the new guys, was using the belt sander on a plank of ironbark timber. Ryan, another newbie, stirred a big tin of weatherproof stain.

Noise was good. It blocked out the annoying voice in Jack's head that tried to tell him Sienna was right—success was trying your best.

Bullshit. Success was enjoying what you do. If he wanted to spend his time playing golf and kayaking and could finance his lifestyle through investments on the proceeds of his previous life, then who was she to complain? He'd restarted the Men's Shed. What more did she want?

"Hey, Jack," a familiar voice called from the door.

"Paul! Good to see you, mate." He gave Paul's suit

and tie the once-over. "I'm guessing you didn't come by for your old job as a bicycle grease monkey."

"No, I've got a position as a planner with parks and recreation."

"Sienna mentioned you had a government job. I knew you wouldn't be out of work for long." Jack threw down his screwdriver. "Want a coffee? Jean brought over a chocolate cake."

"Sorry, can't stay." Paul greeted Ralph and nodded to Brett and Ryan. "I've got a job for the Shed, if you're interested. The council is replacing picnic benches in all the parks in the shire. We need twenty-eight new benches. Think you can handle it?"

"You bet!" Jack said, surprised and pleased. "Thanks, mate. Right now we're building picnic tables on spec but that can be put on hold. When do you want the benches?"

Paul gave him an information sheet on the specs of the project. "It was supposed to go out to tender, so some local contractors won't be happy about losing out on the job. But the committee unanimously agreed that the Men's Shed deserved a one-off boost to help get it going. Can you get the costings to me by next Tuesday, when the committee meets again?"

"Sure thing. We'll need more men, but that shouldn't be a problem. I'm getting a lot of calls from guys interested in joining."

Paul glanced around the shed. "Bob didn't come back?"

"He and his wife opened a stall in Red Hill Market for their kites. They're doing okay."

"How's Sienna?"

"I, uh, haven't seen her for a while."

"Excuse me, Jack?" Ryan said. "There's a man here asking for you."

Jack turned and saw Steve outlined in the doorway, Smedley at his feet. "Dad! You finally made it. Hey, guys, this is my father, Steve."

Jack's grin faded quickly. Steve was gripping the door frame, his heavy belly sagging. His sparse gray hair stood up in wispy tufts and perspiration beaded on his forehead.

"Dad?" Jack strode across to place a hand on his shoulder and peer into the older man's face. "You all right, mate? You don't look well."

"I'm fine." Steve's watery hazel eyes blinked behind his steel-framed glasses. He lifted a shaky hand to wave away Jack's concern. "I'm just a little dizzy. I'll be all right if I sit down for a minute."

Brett and Ryan stopped work and watched uncertainly.

"Can I do anything?" Paul asked, worried.

"No, but thanks," Jack said. "I'll get back to you on the costings."

"Okay." Paul gripped Steve's shoulder. "Take it easy, okay?" Then he left the workshop.

Jack guided his father over to a chair at the kitchen table. His father had shaved badly this morning, leaving behind patches of gray stubble. "Are you sick? Should I call Sienna?"

"No, no. I'm *not* sick," he insisted, laboring for breath. "Just, I walked here. And I haven't eaten yet today. That's why I'm light-headed." Steve rubbed his gnarled knuckles across his pants. His gaze drifted past Jack and settled on the chocolate cake.

"Would you like a piece?" Jack asked. "If you haven't had breakfast your blood sugar's probably low."

"It sure looks good," Steve said, swallowing. "A small piece couldn't hurt."

"I'll get you some coffee to go with it." Jack cut a big wedge of cake and slapped it onto a plate. "There, tuck in to that."

Steve picked up the fork and sliced down through the moist chocolate layers. He scooped up a bite, chewed and swallowed, then followed it quickly with a second bite.

"Is something wrong with your car?" Jack asked. "I can drive you."

"Exercise is supposed to be good for me. I was walking into the village."

"On an empty stomach?" Jack pulled up a chair at the table, trying to figure out what was going on. "Sienna told me a while ago you were having blood tests. What was that about?"

Steve ignored the question and shoveled cake into his mouth. Smedley, nose down, searched the floor for fallen crumbs.

Jack began to drum his fingers on the Formica. Steve's behavior wasn't normal. He didn't look well. His breathing was shallow and rapid and a pulse throbbed visibly in his throat.

Steve held out his empty plate. "More."

"Are you sure that's smart?" Jack asked. "I'll cook you a proper breakfast—porridge, eggs, toast, whatever you like."

Steve blinked and squinted, rubbing at his eyes. "This'll do." He reached for the cake plate and pulled it across the table toward him. And kept pulling…

"Dad!" Jack jumped up.

The plate slid right off the table and crashed to the concrete floor. "Sorry. I thought…" He rubbed at his eyes again. "Peepers…bit blurry."

The other men started forward, but Jack held up a hand. Inside his head, alarm bells were clanging. Steve was sweating profusely now and his skin was a sickly shade of white. "I'm calling Sienna."

"She'll be mad at me."

"Join the club," Jack said, then added, "Why should she be mad at *you?*"

"Those blood tests. Tell her I'm on my way."

"Blood tests for…?"

"Di'betes."

Hell. Jack went cold all over. "What have you been eating since Mum's been away?"

"Cookies, mostly. Lotta ice cream."

Without fuss Jack got up and took Steve's arm, exerting a firm upward pressure. Shards of crockery crunched underfoot as he guided his father, protesting, to the door. "Stow the complaints, mate. I'm taking you straight to the hospital."

"What about Smedley?" Steve said. He stumbled over the doorstep. "I can't leave Smedley alone."

"Don't worry about your dog," Jack said, his fear rising. "I'll look after him."

BEV POKED HER HEAD INSIDE Sienna's office door. "The hospital just rang. Steve Thatcher is in E.R. He's in a diabetic coma."

Sienna stood up so suddenly that her Swiss ball bounced once and rolled away. "What's my schedule like this morning? Can we juggle anyone?"

"You've got Mrs. Bannister at 10:40, but she just called to say she'll be delayed half an hour. Timmy Robinson's here. Natalie could squeeze him in. But you'll have to get back for Mrs. Rothwell. The results of her biopsy are in and I'm sure she'll want to hear the news from you."

Sienna snatched her purse out of a drawer. "I'll be back as soon as I can."

Fifteen minutes later she pulled into the hospital parking lot, grabbed her M.D. tag and ran into the E.R. "Dr. Sienna Maxwell," she informed the blond nurse in reception. "Steve Thatcher is my patient. Where can I find him?"

"Through those doors, down the corridor and second room on your left."

"Thanks." Sienna hurried past the packed waiting room. One bed of the three-bed ward she'd been directed to was occupied by an elderly woman. A young boy with a bandaged head lay in another bed, looking at a book with his mother. In the third bed lay Steve Thatcher.

Steve, gray-faced and eyes shut, had been raised into a sitting position, an IV unit dripping saline into his left hand. Heart rate, oxygen saturation and blood pressure monitors beeped quietly in the background.

Jack sat beside the bed. He hadn't noticed her yet and she had a moment to watch him unguarded. But what she saw scared her. His eyes were hollow and his face drawn. Although his gaze was fixed on his comatose father, he seemed to be looking inward.

Sienna wanted to go to him, to comfort him.

Then he looked up and saw her. The blank hollow look filled with anger and accusation.

Sienna avoided Jack's gaze and kept a tight grip on her emotions. She moved past him to press her fingers to Steve's wrist. Pulse—130. Gently she lifted a thin wrinkled eyelid. His pupil didn't contract. Unresponsive. She moved to the end of the bed to check his chart. The admitting doctor had noted severe dehydration. Steve's blood glucose reading was through the roof.

Finally she turned to Jack. "What happened?"

"He walked over to the Shed and more or less collapsed. Sweating profusely, blurred vision… Why didn't you tell me he had diabetes?"

"Doctor-patient confidentiality. And it was never confirmed. I did try to warn you. Do you know if he's eaten or drunk anything this morning?"

"He hadn't eaten when he got to my place. I gave him a piece of cake—"

"*Cake?* That's the worst thing you could have given him."

"I didn't know! How could you let a man this sick run around?"

"He wasn't this sick when I examined him," Sienna said. "How did he look before he ate the cake?"

"Not great." Jack ran a hand over his face. "As I said, his vision was blurry, he had trouble walking, his breathing was rapid…"

"He must have already been suffering from high blood sugar levels." Sienna chewed on her lip, frowning.

"He told me he'd been eating a lot of cookies and ice cream." Sienna glanced sharply at Jack. "My mother's still away," he explained. "Steve's angry at her."

"This could be a bid to get her to come home," Sienna said, recalling things Steve had said about Hetty. "Have you called her?"

Jack nodded wearily. "The leaders of the retreat wouldn't let me speak to her. She's taking part in five days of silence."

"Give me the number," Sienna said. "I'll talk to them."

"If he was lonely he could have come to my house anytime," Jack said, fishing the scrap of paper out of his wallet. "He knows that."

Sienna took the phone number. "It's Hetty he wants."

"It's bloody childish if you ask me." Jack gazed at his father and shook his head. "If he was trying to punish her it was dumb. He only hurt himself." He turned back to Sienna. "What's going to happen to him?"

"He'll stay in the hospital for a few days until he stabilizes," Sienna said. "The doctors here will check him for damage to his kidneys and retinas. He'll have to go on medication to regulate his blood sugar levels, at least for a while."

"I offered him porridge, eggs..." Jack trailed off, watching his father.

"I should have tried harder to convey my concerns to you." Sienna checked Steve's pulse and blood pressure again. His eyelids fluttered occasionally but stayed closed, his breathing was labored and his fingers twitched now and then. His condition was serious but appeared to be stable. There was nothing more she could do for now. The nurses would monitor him and administer the meds as needed.

Sienna glanced at her watch. "I have to get back to the clinic. I have a cancer patient waiting."

"I'll walk you out," Jack said. "I could use some air."

Sienna retraced her steps through the hospital and out the doors of the E.R. to the parking lot. Jack walked silently at her side. She paused beside her car. "Jack, is there something else?"

"I— Forget it. It's history."

"Tell me. Please." Whether it was for her sake or his that she wanted him to confide in her, she had no idea. She was confused about a lot of things but she knew he was hurting, and that was painful to her.

"Seeing my dad like that, cold and gray as death, brought it all back."

"Brought what back?" she prompted.

"Don't you have a patient?"

"I've got a minute."

"Okay." He drew in a deep breath. "Leanne was pregnant when she died."

Pregnant. Sienna's heart contracted. "Oh, Jack." She slipped her hand into his and squeezed.

"When we left on that flight to Merimbula for the weekend I didn't know," he went on. "She was excited about something and begged to go with me. I tried to put her off because I was testing the GPS and needed to focus on the instruments. But..." He cleared his throat. "She could be so damned persistent."

His face worked as he fought for control. It was a moment before he could continue. "She didn't tell me until we were on the way home. Then I was excited, too. We were making plans, talking and laughing. I didn't pay enough attention to the instrument panel."

Sienna felt his anguish like a physical pain in her chest. "It was an accident. A tragic accident. Life *is* short. Too short to punish yourself."

"I've never told anyone else this," Jack added, sounding bewildered he was doing it now. "The coroner knew, of course, but no one else."

"Why not?"

"Everyone loved Leanne. My sisters, our friends and of course her family. I didn't want to add to anyone's grief. It seemed easier to let the baby die a secret."

"So you've carried this for three years all by yourself?"

He glanced away, blinking.

She raised a hand to his cheek and slowly turned his face until he was forced to meet her gaze. "You didn't kill Leanne. You didn't kill your baby. It's a tragedy, but it's not your fault."

"I know." He dragged in a breath. "I just haven't been able to let it go."

Tears filled her eyes. "You're a good man, Jack. The best."

Suddenly she knew that his occupation, or lack of it, didn't matter to her anymore. She loved him. Whether he ran his own business, won a Nobel Prize, got a bunch of unemployed men interested in life or just kayaked around the bay all day every day.

How could she not have understood that before?

CHAPTER FIFTEEN

THE SUMMERSIDE CEMETERY was deserted when Jack arrived just before sunset. The row of tall cypresses around the perimeter stood starkly black against the pink-and-gold western sky. He'd brought red roses for Leanne and a spray of yellow carnations for the baby.

"Hey, Leanne." He placed the roses, then stood at the foot of the grave with his head bowed in a short prayer. Lifting his head again, he said, "I'm going to put our baby's name on the headstone with yours. I should have done it long ago."

Jack swallowed. "How does Theodore John sound? Those were two of the names we talked about that day—" He broke off, blinking rapidly. "Oh, God," he said, his throat thick. "Forgive me, Leanne."

The wind moved the heavy cypress branches. A magpie called. An answering warble came on the breeze. Jack breathed a deep shuddering sigh and wiped his face with his forearm. "I'll take that as a sign. You always did have a soft spot for those bloody magpies."

He looked at the other bouquet in his hands. "Theodore John, I'm so sorry I never met you. Take care of your mum."

He set the carnations next to the roses and listened as the silence settled over the graveyard. The sun sank below the horizon and the wind died.

After a moment he spoke again. "You know I'll always love you, Leanne. But it's time for me to start again. I think you'd be the first to tell me that. You'd like Sienna. She's fearless about doing what she believes is right." He smiled. "Even when she's wrong."

As he slowly walked away from Leanne's grave he lifted his eyes from the thick green grass to the wide sturdy trunks of the cypresses and their dark spreading limbs. By the time his gaze reached the blue-black sky where the evening star twinkled, he felt almost light enough to fly.

His steps quickened with a new sense of purpose, carrying him back to the Shed. He had work to do.

SIENNA PLACED A BAG OF potatoes in her basket and moved along the vegetable display in the greengrocery. Shopping and cooking for herself wasn't exactly inspirational. Maybe she'd invite Lexie to have dinner with her after her sitting this afternoon. If Lexie wasn't going to Jack's for dinner, that was.

Sienna studied the zucchini, trying to decide whether to buy the green or the yellow variety. Then she heard a rich deep male laugh coming from the other side of the shop. *Jack.* She hadn't seen him since two days ago in the hospital. Or talked to him aside from a brief phone call to say that she'd been able to pass the message to Hetty about Steve's illness.

Furtively she tucked her braided hair over her shoulder and made as little movement as possible so as not to draw attention to herself. Yep, it was him, leaning on his trolley and joking with Mrs. Johnson from the seniors' home as if he hadn't a care in the world. Obviously *he* wasn't nursing a broken heart.

Placing one green and one yellow zucchini in her basket, she circled around behind the central display of cut flowers. If she went through the rear checkout she could slip out through the loading dock without him seeing her.

"Sienna."

She turned slowly, pasting on a smile, steeling herself against those dark intelligent eyes that could be both compassionate and passionate, that ready grin whose crooked curves were full of humor and sex appeal. He wore a fitted shirt that hugged his broad shoulders and tapered to a narrow waist and hips. His thick tousled hair was still damp from a shower—or more likely a swim in the ocean. A stab of pain hit her hard to think of what she'd had and lost.

"Jack!" she said brightly. "Fancy meeting you here."

"My home away from home." He didn't seem to know what to do with his hands.

"Steve's being released from the hospital on Monday," Sienna said. Of course, Jack would know that.

He nodded. "Hetty's coming home on Sunday."

"I hope they sort out their problems."

Several beats went by. She couldn't drag her eyes away from his. Casting about, she came up with a lame "I hear the Men's Shed has a big project."

"News travels fast," Jack said. "Paul only came in with the tender this week."

"Lexie mentioned it when she called to see if I could sit for her this afternoon."

"And are you? Sitting, that is?"

"Yes." Sienna gripped the plastic handle of her basket. "I don't have to wear the toga anymore, thank goodness."

"How's Oliver?"

So. They were going to hit every painful subject before she could get out of here. "He's at his dad's for the term break. But he's coming back to school here. He's finishing grade twelve. And then we'll see."

"Are you happy with that?"

"I can live with it. I'm going to have to if I don't want my son to run away to join the circus."

"I want to thank you for that day in the parking lot," Jack said. "The things you said helped me move on in my life."

"I'm glad." She smiled. "I really better go. Lexie's expecting me."

"It's Saturday. Do you want to come to dinner tonight?"

"I...uh..." She longed to say yes. "Thanks but I've got other plans."

"That's too bad. I was going to make something special."

"Sorry." And she *was* sorry. But that didn't mean she could endure an evening with his friends, pretending she was enjoying herself, all the while aching for what might have been. "Another time."

"Sure."

The way he said it, she knew he wouldn't ask again.

"SO HOW'S JACK?" Lexie squeezed a worm of vermilion paint onto her palette and spread an edge of it into a blob of ocher.

"Fine, I guess." On a dais in the center of the room, Sienna fidgeted on her chair. Lexie had blocked in the toga and was working on the head, so Sienna was thankfully able to stay in her normal clothes. She didn't feel like talking about Jack.

"He said he was going to invite you to dinner tonight." Lexie took a brush and mixed the two colors.

"He did, but I can't go."

"Too bad." Lexie scrutinized her in that unnerving way she had, as if she was looking straight through to Sienna's soul, when in reality she was probably analyzing the distance from her upper lip to the bottom of her nose.

"I've hardly seen him this week," Lexie went on, making a few swift strokes on the canvas. "He's been so busy."

"He got the Men's Shed running again."

"As well as a project of his own he's working on."

"A project?" Sienna repeated, her ears pricking. It really didn't matter to her what he did with his time, as long as he was happy. But just privately, she still believed that having a goal he was working toward would bring him the most satisfaction.

"It's top secret," Lexie said. "He won't even tell me and Renita. But he's been at it night and day."

Could it be the GPS? Sienna wondered with a surge of excitement. "Are *you* going over there for dinner tonight?"

Lexie tossed the rag and loaded up her brush with paint. "He didn't invite me."

"Really." That was odd. "I thought you and Renita had a standing invitation."

Lexie gave her a sly smile. "Maybe he wanted a quiet dinner for two."

"Do you think so? I just assumed there would be the usual crowd." Sienna felt a faint stirring of hope. Maybe she was giving up too easily. But no, he'd been so angry at her over Olly. She wondered what he would say if she told him Oliver really had cheated. But she wouldn't do that to Olly. Loyalty was important to her, too.

Lexie motioned her to move to the left. "Turn just a little...that's good."

From her new vantage point Sienna saw a flash of dark hair pass the window. Her heart kicked into overdrive. Then it dropped back into low gear as Renita knocked and entered.

"Hey, ladies," Renita said. "Hope you don't mind, Lexie. Jack told me Sienna was going to be here and I wanted to ask her about the latest on Dad."

"You're forgiven this time," Lexie said.

Renita turned to Sienna. "Is he going to be okay?"

"He's had a scare, but he'll be fine."

"That's a relief." Renita removed a stack of empty frames from a chair and sat. "What's the deal with his condition? Can you fill us in so we can help him get healthy?"

Sienna gave them a brief rundown on type 2 diabetes. "Once he gets his blood sugar stabilized, it's mainly diet and exercise."

"Mum will have to help him watch his diet," Renita said. "And I'm sure Jack will make him exercise."

"It's up to Dad to make sure he's doing the right thing," Lexie said. "Mum's got her own life."

"How do you think he got to this state?" Renita argued. "She took off and left him."

"Lexie's right," Sienna inserted quickly. "Steve needs to understand his condition and take responsibility. But—" she nodded to Renita "—Hetty can help and encourage him."

"If their marriage holds up," Lexie said quietly.

"I had no idea they were having problems," Renita agreed, subdued. "You just expect your parents to always be there, like the furniture."

"Hetty will be home soon," Sienna said, trying to put an optimistic spin on the situation. "That's a good start."

"I'd better go," Renita said, looking at her watch. "I've got a hot date." She grinned as she rose and salsa'd the few steps to the door. "I'm going dancing."

So she wasn't going to Jack's, either, Sienna thought. Could Lexie be right, that Jack had planned a special dinner for two?

Lexie glanced at the clock. "Is it that late? No wonder the light is fading. Sienna, we'll have to finish for today."

"That's okay." Sienna slipped her jacket on and gathered her purse. "I've got to go anyway."

"What are you doing tonight?" Lexie asked.

"I'm not sure." But she wasn't going home to her empty house to eat potatoes and zucchini.

Her problem, she mused as she drove across town, was that she kept underestimating Jack. Look at the way he'd reacted to the phony dinner she'd served at her party. He hadn't been angry at her then for not being perfect. So why did she think he would give up on her now? He'd said he loved her in spite of her flaws. She had to find out if he really meant it. That no matter what stupid thing she did today he'd still be with her tomorrow. Even Erica thought that if he loved her, he would forgive her.

It was only five o'clock. It wouldn't even be dark for a couple hours yet. Way too soon to arrive for dinner, but if she was wrong and other guests were coming she had some things she wanted to say before the hordes descended.

Words and explanations were tumbling through her mind, so she didn't notice right away that Jack was coming out of his driveway at the same time as she turned in. She slammed on the brakes, almost crashing head-on into his utility truck.

Sienna waited a moment until her heartbeat slowed. Then, deliberately, she turned off the ignition and pulled on the hand brake. Jack Thatcher wasn't going anywhere.

Jack climbed out of his ute to check the front end. Their bumpers were just touching. "You're damn lucky."

"*I'm* lucky? *You* almost scratched my chrome." This wasn't quite the way she'd envisaged sweet-talking her way back into his life.

"Did you want something?" he asked. "I'm in a hurry."

He wasn't making this any easier. But she was here, she was going to see it through. Sienna sucked in a breath. "The thing is, I'm not perfect."

He stared at her. "Whoever asked you to be perfect?"

"I've been less than truthful at times." She sped on before she lost her nerve. "I can't cook to save my soul. I'm too demanding of other people—" She broke off. "This is embarrassing. Aren't you going to stop me?"

"Nope." He crossed his arms over his chest and leaned against the hood of his vehicle, a small smile playing over his face. "Go on—this is interesting."

"I've lost my train of thought." She frowned and muttered, "You know I've never admitted any of this to anyone before. You might be a little nicer."

"Okay, I'll help. You're a workaholic."

"High achiever."

"Competitive."

"That can be a *good* thing."

"Stubborn." He took a step forward, hands on hips.

"Determined." She tossed her head.

"You have a temper." He was nose-to-nose with her.

"I'm *passionate*." Her fists were clenched at her sides.

"I *know*." He wrapped his arms around her waist and lifted her for a bruising kiss.

She was out of comebacks. Unless throwing her arms around his neck and deepening the kiss counted as a witty riposte. Finally he loosened his hold and she slid boneless to the ground.

"What just happened here?" she said, dazed. Their arms still encircled each other.

"It's called making up," he said into her hair, his husky voice making her shiver deliciously.

"I wasn't finished talking."

"You were finished." He kissed her temple. "I've got a lifetime to discover your imperfections. There's no rush."

A lifetime. A thrill went through her. "So you'll take me as I am?"

"Do I have a choice?" His voice softened. "I love you. I'll never stop loving you."

She lifted her face for another long, lingering kiss. Breaking apart, she said, "Let's take this inside."

"Can't." He looked past her at the sky. "I have to go. You can wait here for me or I'll come by your place when I'm done."

"Where are you going? Can I come?"

"You wouldn't want to. Anyway, it's something I need to do on my own."

"Why are you being so cagey? Tell me what it is."

"I'm going to take my plane up and test the GPS."

Her eyes widened. She wanted to leap at him and hug him but made herself ask casually, "So you've fixed it?"

He nodded. "I'm going to fly into the sunset over the bay. That used to be my favorite thing."

Sienna swallowed. "Then it's going to be my favorite thing, too. I'm coming."

"But you're afraid of flying in small planes. You'll have a panic attack."

"Do I look like a woman who's okay with her weaknesses, or do I look like a woman who wants to overcome them?"

"The GPS might still have problems. This is a test run."

"It's a clear evening, not a breath of wind. We're not

going to hit anything or crash. And I promise I won't say a word to distract you."

"It might not work," he repeated. "There may be no future in it."

Ah, now she knew what he was trying to say. "Jack, I don't give a flying fig whether it works or not, except for your sake. Just as I don't care what you do as long as I can be with you, and be part of your life. Not just for one night, or one month or one year. But for always."

Maybe it was the rich glow of the westering sun shining in his face or maybe she'd said the right thing for once, because Jack seemed to light up from within. "Okay, then. Let's go."

JACK REMOVED THE BLOCKS from behind the wheels of the Whitney Boomerang he'd borrowed for the test and climbed into the pilot's seat. Next to him in the copilot's seat Sienna had her head between her knees and was breathing into a paper bag.

He performed the instrument checks, paying particular attention to setting up the GPS program. He'd installed it the day before, so he was ready in minutes.

He rubbed his hand over Sienna's back. Speaking through the headphones, he asked, "Are you sure you want to do this?"

She sat up, pushing her hair back and adjusting her headphones over her ears. Her face was white, but she managed to smile and give him a thumbs-up. "I'm sure."

Jack turned on the two-way radio and gave the control tower his call sign. "Whitney Boomerang XR6J, ready for takeoff. Over."

"Permission to take off, XR6J. Over," came the crackling reply.

Jack pushed on the joystick and the single-wing airplane taxied over the bumpy ground toward the runway. He glanced across at Sienna. Her eyes were scrunched shut, her body rigid and her nostrils flared with each breath. She had guts, he'd give her that.

Now he was at the end of the runway, engine thrumming, propeller whirring, fuselage vibrating. He was nervous, too, but the three years since he'd flown fell away and every detail of procedure came flooding back to him. Even so, he tamped down his excitement to ensure he didn't miss a single step in the preflight routine. The movements of his hands on the controls, his feet on the rudder pedals, the alertness of his gaze—all his training and instincts were still there, solid.

He started slowly down the tarmac, straightened the plane out, then increased his speed. He glanced at the GPS. The coordinates of the airfield were showing correctly. So far, so good. The end of the runway approached in a rush. One eye on the tachometer, Jack increased the revs, tilted the elevator on the horizontal stabilizer…

And they were airborne.

The pressure in his chest lifted as the small plane climbed up, up, over the rolling hills and valleys, orchards and paddocks of the peninsula. Banking, he worked the rudder pedals and made a clean sweeping curve west toward the blue sparkling waters of Port Phillip Bay. The glass panels of the city high-rises fringing the bay glinted gold. White sand beaches were blue with shadow. The first pink streaks of the setting sun were etched across the gilded sky.

"Do you know you're grinning from ear to ear?" Sienna asked.

Now that she'd mentioned it, he realized his face was sore from smiling. "Are you okay?"

Sienna's fists were white-knuckled in her lap, but her eyes were open. "It's a whole other world up here."

He flew her high over beaches, low over a pod of leaping dolphins, inspected a dredger in the shipping channel, circled a cruise ship heading out to sea and buzzed a flotilla of sailing dinghies near the marina.

His flight path wasn't as random as it probably appeared to Sienna. He'd filed it with the air traffic controller before leaving, and at every phase of the trip he checked and double-checked the route adherence monitor and GPS signals.

Now for the most important test of all. He switched off the satellite receiver on the GPS. The day of the crash it had started behaving like a simulator, masking the fault that had led to Leanne's death.

"Did you see those pelicans!" Sienna exclaimed, her nose pressed to the window, gaping at the large ungainly birds flapping past at eye level.

"Shh." Jack raised a hand.

"Sorry." She mimed zipping her lips.

His gaze fixed on the GPS screen, he banked the plane and turned in the opposite direction to his prescribed flight path. He held his breath until his lungs were begging for oxygen. *Come on, come on...*

Beep, beep, beep. The tiny airplane on the GPS screen flashed on and off, alerting him to the fault.

Letting his breath out in a gusty sigh of relief, he flicked the satellite receiver back on and reset the flight path.

"Is something wrong?" Sienna asked. "Not that I'm worried or anything."

"Nothing's wrong. In fact, everything's terrific!" Jack laughed out loud. "The GPS is working perfectly. Hang on to your hat!" He tilted the nose of the plane straight up, and up…and over backward in a loop-the-loop that had Sienna screaming like a teenager on a roller coaster.

When they were flying level and steady again he expected to receive a blast for scaring her. Instead Sienna turned to him, her eyes huge and her hair a ruffle of red ringlets framing her face. "That was awesome!"

Jack laughed again, a full-throated eruption from deep in his gut. Sienna yanked off her headphones and held her ears. If he hadn't been afraid she'd start screaming again he would have put the plane on autopilot and kissed her.

Instead he banked once more and circled above Summerside. An unexpected pride and fierce love for his little town tightened his chest as he pointed out the various landmarks to Sienna. There was the beach where she'd kayaked out to meet him, the cliff-top road they'd jogged along. A little farther inland Sienna's tiled roof was just visible below the treetops. There was the creek that ran behind Lexie's studio, and the village commercial district with the clinic, the greengrocer, Renita's bank and a host of other shops and restaurants. Five blocks east was the high school where they'd played trivia. To the south, past another winding creek, were the corrugated metal rooftops of Jack's house and the Men's Shed next door.

Sienna sniffled and her eyes were shining. "I love this place."

He smiled, his heart full. *I love you.*

Then there were more paddocks and roads and trees and a glimpse of Western Port Bay on the other side of the peninsula. A deep sense of contentment filled Jack as he guided the little aircraft home to the airfield. And when the wheels touched down on the runway, he had to take a few deep breaths to control his emotions.

He had his life back.

He taxied back to the hangar and parked the aircraft. Shutting down the engine, he unstrapped himself and climbed out, telling Sienna to wait there. Going around the plane, he opened the door for her and helped her down. She swung into his arms and for a moment he held her in a wordless embrace.

Correction. He had a *new* life. Thanks to his red-haired Venus de Milo. He could see turbulence ahead, and at times it would be a bumpy ride because they didn't always agree. But that was okay. They were both in it for the long haul.

"Come on, love," he said. "Let's go home."

* * * * *

COMING NEXT MONTH

Available February 8, 2011

#1686 THE LAST GOODBYE
Going Back
Sarah Mayberry

#1687 IN HIS GOOD HANDS
Summerside Stories
Joan Kilby

#1688 HIS WIFE FOR ONE NIGHT
Marriage of Inconvenience
Molly O'Keefe

#1689 TAKEN TO THE EDGE
Project Justice
Kara Lennox

#1690 MADDIE INHERITS A COWBOY
Home on the Ranch
Jeannie Watt

#1691 PROMISE TO A BOY
Suddenly a Parent
Mary Brady

HSRCNM0111

Spotlight on

Classic

Quintessential, modern love stories
that are romance at its finest.

See the next page
to enjoy a sneak peek from
the Harlequin® Romance series.

CATCLASSHR10

want to ask the questions now pulsing through his mind. But then he remembered the old saying—*Don't look a gift horse in the mouth.* He'd benefit from whatever insight she had and be glad of it.

"I don't really know what babies need," he said. "I fed her, patted her back like you did, walked her to sleep, but every time I put her down…"

Wyatt almost groaned. Of course. He'd forgotten one important thing. He'd been so focused on getting the formula the right temperature that he'd forgotten to check her diaper. Not that he had any clue what to do there either.

Pulling calves and shoveling out stalls was far less intimidating than one tiny newborn.

"She's probably due for a diaper change, isn't she." He tried to sound nonchalant. This was a perfect opportunity. Elli must know how to change a diaper. He could simply watch her so he'd know better for the next time.

Instead, Elli came around the corner of the counter and placed Darcy back in his arms. "Here you go, Uncle Wyatt," she said lightly. "You get diaper duty. I'll fix the coffee. Cream and sugar?"

Oh boy, Wyatt thought, looking down into Darcy's pursed face, his smug plan blown to smithereens. He was in for it now.

Will sparks fly between Elli and Wyatt?

Find out in
PROUD RANCHER, PRECIOUS BUNDLE

Available February 2011 from Harlequin Romance

HREXP0211